This book is a work of fiction. References to real people, actual events, existing   organizations, and specific locations are made only to provide a sense of reality typical in works of fiction. References to other people, other events, other organizations, and other locations are all the product of the author's imagination. Any resemblance to real people, actual events, existing organizations, and specific locations are entirely accidental, and the author has sought to be careful to avoid such mishaps. If any resemblance is found, it reflects a mistake on the part of the author, not an intended disparagement.

# I RETRIBUTION

The Bentley Continental GT inched out of the garage adjacent to the securitized manor house of Sir Roger Gilchrest, located approximately thirty miles to the South West of central London and commonly referred to by the locals as Fort Gilchrest. The car had been customized to Sir Roger's own specifications and was his pride and joy. As CEO of a large financial company, SNCH, he thought he owed it to his shareholders and employees, and indeed the nation, to ensure his own safety against every threat in these times of widespread hostility to bankers. Thus, the car was bullet proof and bomb proof. One centimeter thick steel and even thicker glass meant that no rifle or pistol bullet would penetrate, and the special curtain of vertical metallic blinds that lowered instantly whenever the car slowed below ten miles an hour ensured that no bomb could be easily placed underneath the car. The possibility of a limpet explosive device being attached on the outside of the car while being driven, perhaps by the rider of a motorbike, had been undermined by a special plastic covering over all the metal and glass that guaranteed no magnetic or adhesive attachment would function. Nor could the car be easily crushed, either horizontally or vertically, owing to the many steel struts inserted into the frame of the car.

As a further precaution the air supply inside the car could be made independent of that outside by switching on two oxygen canisters that would keep a person alive for up to five hours. And, if the tires were shot out, the car could still speed away at up to eighty miles an hour on its wheels alone. Naturally, all the windows were heavily tinted, precluding those outside the car from seeing inside. Moreover, if for any reason an unforeseen threat did materialize, Sir Roger had been licensed to carry two semi-automatic pistols and an automatic shotgun inside the car (a special privilege secured through the intervention of the Prime Minister himself). Naturally, all the armour added considerable weight to the car, but had been adequately compensated for by the installation of a much more powerful engine and an enhanced braking system, so that its overall performance was hardly affected. Given the complementary systems of protection in the manor house, his office building, and virtually all of the places he would visit, Sir Roger felt close to being invulnerable, and, while the cost had been huge, it was paid by his bank and was, of course, a tax-deductible expense.

Sir Roger himself also matched his vehicle. He was a large man, with large appetites and large resources to satisfy them. On this Friday morning, he was behind the wheel, driving to the House of Commons where he had an appointment with the Chancellor of the Exchequer at 10.15 a.m. This was certainly the best place for such a meeting because there would be no Treasury officials present, some of whom would certainly resist Sir Roger's proposals. Indeed, it was new regulatory ideas emerging from the bureaucrats that had led to him requesting the meeting 'one on one'. Sir Roger, like many other bankers, regarded regulation as appropriate only if it improved profitability by reducing competition, qualifying the rights of customers, lowering capital requirements, or eliminating similar impediments to the creation of 'value', and it was precisely a new set of such restrictions on these matters that had been proposed by finance specialists in the Treasury. Sir Roger was determined to ensure that they would never see the light of day. He was especially worried by proposals to tighten up the enforcement of laws targeting money laundering by substantially increasing the fines on financial institutions for processing, so called, dirty money. This would seriously reduce profits and his own bonuses. While he admitted sometimes in private conversations with other bankers that the evidence was strong that these money flows facilitated the operations of international criminal gangs, rogue regimes, the bribing of politicians and terrorism, his public stance was one hundred and eighty degrees different and he proposed that nothing needed to be done. Hopefully, there would also be time to raise the matter of the privatization of the National Health Service. He knew that several senior members of the government were supportive of the scheme, and he wanted to add the weight of the 'banking community' behind the proposal. They would, of course, be suitably rewarded for the financial engineering involved in the changes of ownership and also by the interest paid on loans made to the new privatized entities.

He was confident of his success as he knew the Chancellor well. They had been at Eton and Oxford together, met socially quite frequently, and he knew that he could be very persuasive when it came to explaining the intricacies of 'value analysis'. Moreover, he was himself one of the funnels in which financial contributions of the City – the term typically used to refer to the area in London where the headquarters of the major banks and other financial institutions had located – were made to all political parties and members of parliament. He could also hold out the prospect of a lucrative set of directorships once the Chancellor had completed his ministerial term. No doubt the American system of government was easier to work with because of the ease with which lobbying could be undertaken in a system lacking less strict party discipline, yet with a powerful legislature and phenomenally expensive elections which made campaign contributions especially valuable. However, he was lumbered with the British system that also required a more subtle approach. This involved expounding the belief that what was good for the City was good for the nation as a whole, and that only leftist malcontents, power-hungry bureaucrats, and unworldly liberals contested this for their own special interests.

Sir Roger had risen to his present position in the aftermath of the 2008 financial crisis more by luck than good judgment. Prior to the crisis, he was head of mergers and acquisitions and, therefore, had been spared the embarrassment of being responsible for acquiring derivatives which turned toxic. Not that Sir Roger thought that his colleagues in the bank to be actually responsible for these mistakes which had brought on the financial crisis. If there was any fault, it lay with governments who were always encouraging banks to lend to the lower classes and small enterprises that really had no business having either assets or liabilities. And in his view, this was again the source of the most recent crisis two months earlier. But, in any event, he believed fervently that some episodes of financial difficulties were inevitable in any productive economy and constituted the principal episodes of creative destruction whereby the weak succumbed to the stronger. The job of government in such circumstances was to preserve the strong, and he took his own rise to the very top in the bank over his more tarnished rivals as evidence of this process of natural selection.

After his meeting with the Chancellor, he would lunch with some colleagues in other financial companies at his own private restaurant in the global headquarters of SNCH. They would discuss the results of his meeting and plan strategy accordingly. He expected even less difficulties here because they all thought alike, and in the event of any difference in emphasis tended to defer to Sir Roger. The truth of the matter was that the invited CEOs knew only generalities and had little idea about most of the specialisms that were part and parcel of the organizations they supposedly managed. And the generalities they expressed constituted the same sort of shallow clichés that Sir Roger spouted about value, although they were rather less eloquent than Sir Roger himself and thus acceded to him. Any mistakes they made would not be especially harmful to themselves. They were all immensely wealthy, their financial companies were seen by the government as too big to fail, and the laws sufficiently vague that the batteries of lawyers they could muster would see off any charge of fraud or dereliction of corporate duties. So it had been in the aftermath of the 2008 crisis, so it would be again in the aftermath of the new crisis two months ago. Nonetheless, it was wise to be cautious and ensure that bankers remained in control of whatever changes materialized.

When his lunch meeting ended, he would drive round to the apartment of his sister-in-law in Kensington, where they would entertain each other carnally until dinner. This was, he recognized, his one security vulnerability that day, but he was willing to take the risk. Rosalind not only had all the requisite physical attributes, but was also intelligent, well informed and amusing to be with. He never failed to find her phrase "a good rogering by Sir Roger" very funny as well as exciting. His brother was an unimpressive creature in each and every way, and he felt no guilt for his fraternal betrayal. In itself, this was one reason for Lady Gilchrest to regard her husband as a "shit of the first order," but, as a matter of fact, she had many other grounds for her indictment, not the least of which was his self-serving notions of 'value' along with the ruthless prosecution of his interests.

As it would transpire, there were others who

tended to think the same way and had the means to make their views take an eventful turn. Sir Roger was in fact a marked man whose dramatic elimination was regarded as a priority by The Committee. His assassination was to be the first.

Twenty minutes into his journey, he had to slow and stop behind a line of two other cars. He could see some smoke rising from around the next bend and assumed that there must have been an accident. This was annoying, but he had plenty of time to spare, and he could see a police officer walking in his direction conferring individually with the drivers of each car in front, so he knew he would soon be put in the picture and could easily change his route from the B2212 if the delay was going to be substantial. Within a couple of minutes, the constable approached the Bentley, and Sir Roger retracted the window into the door on the driver's side of the car. The policeman bent slightly, placed his gloved right hand on top of the door into which the window had been drawn, and began to speak in the customary style, "Good morning sir; unfortunately, I have to inform you that there will be a slight delay to your journey today," and with that his right hand shot forward to the neck of Sir Roger, slicing the trachea completely with the razor sharp circular blade held in the glove between his thumb and index finger. Consciousness was lost almost immediately, and death followed very soon afterwards, but not before a huge amount of blood spurted all over the luxurious interior of the car.

The assassin, confidant that the execution was without flaw, did not wait for final expiry. He delayed departure from the Bentley only long enough to unlock the car door, raise the window and then close the door, which relocked the car automatically, before wiping away most of the blood on himself. He then walked to the car at the front of the line, got in and signaled the driver to lead the other car away. Opening the glove compartment, the phone was found, the call made, and then the phone destroyed. Finally, being able to relax, he looked forward to a well-deserved break from work financed with the large deposit that would shortly be made into his account. It might take a little time, of course, because the death of Sir Roger would not be confirmed for many hours after the car was located. In fact, as it turned out, the emergency services had the devil's own job in gaining entry, thus ironically paying a final tribute to the foresight of at least some of Sir Roger's security precautions.

It had been a straightforward operation for the assassin, albeit a little peculiar in commission. Seven weeks earlier, he had received a call from someone who knew his profession, his curriculum vitae, his menu of fees and many other details of his life. But he had no idea who he was talking to. It was certainly not one of his usual brokers, and, despite his suspicions, he could not help being impressed by the 'good faith' shown by the subsequent deposit of twenty thousand dollars into his Cayman's account when he consented to take the contract. He was periodically updated as to the date and modality of dispatch, the activation signal, and how many of his team he would likely require, along with the assurance that he could keep the initial transfer of money if the project was aborted. As he said to himself at the time, while he always guaranteed value, "You couldn't be fairer than that."

****

The same morning as that of Sir Roger's demise, Rory Candiman awoke at the stroke of nine with an aching body and a severe headache. But truth be said, the previous evening had been fantastic, certainly one of the best he could recall. And he had many memorable occasions. As Vice President for Client Services at Floydsons, a large financial company providing a multitude of services, he was in charge of all entertainment and gifts for clients. This ranged from the distribution of trinkets for ordinary depositors to the much more elaborate and exciting offerings to the bank's substantial investors, such as heads of pension funds and the like who used the bank to manage their portfolios. Typically, the latter took place in a huge apartment in a Kensington hotel that was rented by the bank.

The job was not always easy. There were indeed two principal difficulties which consumed much of his time and energy. He had to discern the likes and dislikes of the clientele, especially of the upper ranks, and if they were shameful or heavily repressed this could be difficult. Of course, some were not. Most of the Arab Sheiks from the Gulf were open about being interested in three things – women, alcohol, and food – so meeting their needs was uncomplicated. Of course, this was not because they had been brought up in a libertarian fashion. Quite the reverse, it reflected the contempt in which they held things western, and especially western women. But most of the other clients tended to be tight-lipped as to their enjoyments in life, and he had to use all of his considerable skills in the charm department to elicit what they *really* liked and disliked. Some of these preferences were innocent enough, and Rory had a wide array of offerings at his disposal. There were the staples, such as tickets to major sports features, plays in the West End, or London's various musical offerings, which usually followed either lunch or dinner at one of the many excellent restaurants available. Next on the list, and somewhat more expensive, were the provision of mini vacations in exotic locations either owned or rented by the company for this purpose and, in fairness it should be said, as getaways for senior executive policy formulation retreats. Then there were the offerings in darker territory. Introductions to attractive women willing to provide 'full girlfriend services', or visits to gay bars for those inclined in the other direction, were the baseline provisions in this register. But from there, it was down and down. In all cases, Rory's job was to ascertain preferences and provide the appropriate satisfactions, and any mistake involving a mismatch of inclinations and outlets could prove expensive if it led to a switch of business to another company by an embarrassed or infuriated client.

The second difficulty came from some of his colleagues. They would sometimes try to dump low yielding investments into the portfolios of the clients. This was a temptation of most traders, but the worst offenders were in the derivatives departments. They could design customized and extraordinarily complex instruments, the most likely value of which could only be ascertained if one had access to the computerized risk models of a major financial company, and the clients had no such knowledge. With a suitable marketing exercise, and some degree of naiveté on the part of purchasers, they could be made to pay hugely in excess of the expected value as determined by the quants in Floydsons. And since in normal times the risk models were not far off mark, these derivatives proved hugely profitable for the bank at the cost, of course, of the clients. In effect, there was something of a civil war going on inside the bank, as one section behaved in ways that shafted the others in order to improve their own bonuses. Rory had to pick up the pieces when it became obvious to the customers he dealt with that they had been conned. Sometimes he could negotiate lower losses for them, but typically the problem also had to be dealt with in the form of some special entertainment which not only satisfied the client's least reputable needs and wildest fantasies but did so while allowing the possibility of blackmail if the client nevertheless proved motivated to switch their business elsewhere.

However, Rory's job was also made easier by the fact

that he was given a free hand and did not have to account in any detail for the monies spent. For the most part, Floydsons did not know and did not want to know any details of expenditures by him. This was not the typical treatment afforded to their executives, but in the case of Rory it was thought to be the wise thing to do.

The outbreak of Covid 19 in 2020, of course, had also been a setback to some of his activities. Many sports arenas, concert halls, theatres, restaurants, and other public places had been shut down so offerings in these facilities were not possible. However, maintaining the supply and demand of the darker pleasures proved to be more robust than he had initially imagined. On reflection, though, this was not altogether surprising. Not only had the pandemic brought an end to many ordinary enjoyments, so generating a buildup of desires, what he had on offer did not centre on mouth to mouth contact so other connections could be readily substituted. Of course, ideally masks had to be worn, but many of his guests actually came to prefer this, not only in order to ensure anonymity but because it added to the pleasures resulting from the many transgressions undertaken. Indeed, some of his clients continued to favour the wearing of masks even though it was no longer necessary after the vaccine had been developed. So, he mused, there could be a silver lining in many a dark cloud.

More generally, life had been exceedingly kind to Rory. Born into a loving middle-class family, reasonably well educated, moderately intelligent, very athletic and exceptionally good looking, he had no disposition to complain in any way. His normal inclination was to work hard so that everyone enjoyed themselves, and he was easily able to exempt himself from the constraints of conventional morality in doing so. Consequently, there were few self-imposed limits, and he invariably found his job interesting and agreeable. Perhaps more importantly, he was very good at it, and this was reflected in the large salary and bonuses he drew every year, even when the company itself was not doing very well, as in the crisis of 2008 and also after the recent repeat two months earlier. Then and now, he had managed to keep most of the large clients and investors placated in the face of the very substantial losses they faced. Subsequently, after the 2008 crisis had passed many expressed their gratitude, not only for the entertainments he had lavished on them, but also because of the recovery of the equities and bond markets in the following years. This had been brought about courtesy of government policies, including subsidies of one kind or another that had moderated and sometimes reversed their initial losses. Hopefully, the same would turn out to be true with the recent financial crisis. He even believed that he had many of his clients' loyalties although he was never silly enough to act as if were so; after all he was integrated sufficiently into the banking industry to realize that such assumptions could prove costly to anyone connected to finance. Thus, he trusted only that the same sort of measures ensuring continuity for the City would be repeated in the face of the contractionary effects of the current difficulties, and he would be able to carry on his job without too much disruption.

However, this morning, despite his bodily ailments, his thoughts were overwhelmed by the pleasures of the previous evening. It had gone superbly. The three clients and the four women he had procured had got on well, or at least had pretended to, and each and every man, including himself, had been energized and completely uninhibited. The excellent food and wine at the start of the evening had put everyone in a good mood, and the drugs had done the rest, overriding any restraint that might still have been present as well as energizing all. So, he lay in bed for a few minutes recollecting the debauchery. He had no qualms at all. No one had been hurt and everything was a matter of 'acts between consenting adults'. Indeed, for some people matters were even better than this as he thought focused on Jimmy Crawford, a little Scotsman with inverted bow-legs, a potbelly, a bum-shaped face and pock-marked skin, who had been especially active. How else would such an unattractive man be able to experience the joys of uninhibited sex with beautiful women? And since all his sexual partners had been generously remunerated, who could object?

Rory's conceptual equipment obviously failed him here as he never factored in the lowered financial returns received by the holders of assets in the funds managed by Jimmy, nor the corrosive effect his actions might have on business and cultural norms. But there were alternative social accounting conventions adhered to by others, including The Committee, which he might have learned of in the future but for the fact that he had only had few minutes left to live. His was to be the second assassination.

The musings on the night before were cut short by Rory remembering that the cleaners were due to arrive at 9.45. He eased himself out of bed and headed for one of the showers. Emerging into the lounge ten minutes later and toweling himself roughly, he heard the door to the apartment open, and two women in the uniforms of the cleaning agency walked into the room. "There must be some mistake", he shouted, "you are not due for another fifteen minutes." He need not have been concerned about any mix up that had taken place. While the shorter of the two moved in front of him and began to explain that the work order clearly stated that it was for a 9.30 a.m. start, the taller one expertly slipped a steel wire garrotte around Rory's neck and tightened immediately. The one in front of Rory then promptly pinned his arms in a bear hug to minimize resistance. He lost consciousness almost immediately and was dead within three minutes, although the garrotte remained in place for a further two minutes after the pulse was lost. The women then removed the wire, packed their uniforms into a large briefcase and computer bag, redressed and tidied themselves up. The call was made, the phone destroyed, the transfer of funds would follow, and their exit made. No one thought it at all unusual as two businesswomen came out of the tower and opened the door of a waiting car.

***

James Stewart was just about definable as having upper middle-class roots. He came from a 'good' family who were moderately wealthy and sought to equip their children with what was necessary to maintain their family's status. James had been sent to two of the best private schools in England and with extensive supplementary tutoring during the long holidays had managed to gain entrance to Oxford, although there were always rumours that strings had been pulled too. While there he had worked quite hard and gained second class honours in modern greats (philosophy, politics, and economics), although he did not particularly like any of these subjects and found most of economics particularly difficult. After graduating, he had initially entertained the thought of a political career and even applied to be a parliamentary candidate in a local conservative riding, but nothing came of it. Instead, he ended up in the City and now, twenty-five years later, headed his own hedge fund – Global Strategy. This provided an annual income of around five million pounds, resulting from fees charged to his investors and a twenty percent share of all profits. And even after a bitter and expensive divorce two years earlier, the fund had allowed him to accumulate a wealth portfolio of approximately twenty million pounds.

James most certainly had his strengths. He was always tenacious and usually charming and, when required, could be vicious. In short, he typified a definition of an English gentleman as 'someone who never *unintentionally* inflicts pain on others'. One result was that he had a large network of acquaintances and contacts, and it was this that was the real foundation of his wealth. Not to put a too fine a point on the matter, he used insider-information extensively. This had allowed him to emerge unscathed through the crisis of 2008 and was again proving its worth in the recent crisis two months earlier. In the former, one of his 'enablers', as he called them, had informed him in late August of that year that Lehman Brothers was on the brink of bankruptcy, well before it became public knowledge. Then, when bankruptcy came to be expected, he had used other 'enablers' to find out before any announcements were made that neither the Federal Reserve nor the US Treasury would do what was necessary to prop up the institution. These two pieces of information had allowed him to take positions that protected his fund from losses, and instead brought significant profits, which in turn, and much to his satisfaction, had been the beginning of his personality cult as the sharpest 'hedgy' in the City. He was employing the same tactics at present to manage the aftermath of the crisis that had broken out two months earlier. The Covid pandemic had been handled in much the same way. His enablers had provided him with fore knowledge of many government policies of support for businesses, and he was able to profit substantially as a result.

Today, James had taken the day off to practice his golf at the Lanchester course, twenty or so miles south of his home in central London. It was a highly exclusive club of which he was a director, and where he could command the course for his sole use for the first hour in the morning of every Friday. What was different today was that he was both elated and annoyed. The elation came from knowing that since the new financial crisis he had 'earned' two million pounds, again resulting from his special talent of locating sources with inside information on future financial happenings who could be persuaded to share it for an appropriate consideration. In the matter just completed, the source was a high-ranking Eurocrat located at the European Central Bank (ECB) who passed on information concerning the plan to sell German bonds and buy Italian, allowing James to take a position long in the latter and short in the former, so benefiting hugely when the subsequent action of the ECB reduced the prices of German bonds and raised those of Italian bonds. It was a simple and brilliant example of James specialism, and far more reliable than the mathematical models of risk that governed the activities of many other hedge funds. Moreover, James was in no doubt that his gains were deserved. In his own view, he was a man of genuine talent, and Britain would be ill-advised not to incentivize 'wealth creators' such as himself. It needed real skills to locate people with valuable information, persuade them that you were legitimate and not an *agent provocateur*, continually reassure them that you could be trusted, and in turn accurately assess their trustworthiness. James could do all this very, very well, and, he deduced, earned a valid remuneration for employing these scarce skills.

The fact that his gains were purely redistributional and illegal were not thoughts that James engaged with of his own volition and nor did his friends in the banking community ever raise difficult questions either in the abstract or the particular. The culture hinged on a singularity – money was the measure of all value, and financial gains themselves evidenced value creation. The Committee knew this very well, but even so were themselves surprised at the pervasiveness of the failure to distinguish private profitability from social productivity. It was, after all, an elementary distinction, well known to most economists since at least Adam Smith. Thus, they had to conclude that the need for self-legitimating illusions was but another deficiency of those inhabiting the institutions of modern finance.

James annoyance also had a concrete source. His usual caddie had texted to say that he had broken his leg and recommended a replacement, whose character and competence he had no hesitation in attesting. But this was a change that was far from minor in James's world, which now comprised only four activities: nourishing his networks, money-making, golf and sex. The latter two, both paid for, were thought of by James as a reward for the money-making, so any success would soon be followed by a round on his favourite course, followed later by a sampling from his long list of escorts. Given his monumental financial gains, he expected all to be perfect, but now was confronted with a rather reserved, and some might say aloof, new caddie who spoke with a French accent that James found particularly irritating. Not that the man did not know his business. On the previous three holes his assessment and advice had been faultless, and James was playing rather better than normal. But he felt distinctly uncomfortable without his usual companion.

This discomfiture was to be well founded, although not for the reasons then evident to James. And, indeed, he would never be in a position to comprehend them. The Committee had put a claim on his life too. His was to be the third assassination.

They were now approaching the third hole, which lay along the diagonal of a large Z shaped cutting through the trees. The start was somewhat into the diagonal and the green lay quite a bit short of the other end. But it was no easy task to play well. The green lay over a hump in the ground and was not completely observable, the width of the grass between the two wooded sides was narrow, and the winds could be strong, as they were today. James was hesitant. The caddie was not, handing James the driver iron along with the recommendation to hit the ball hard and aim fifteen degrees to the right of centre in order to counter the wind. Although rather more precise, this concurred with James's own thoughts, and he set about concentrating on the execution. Unfortunately for James and perhaps for his investors and enablers as well as his mother, but surely for no one else, another execution intervened. While he was concentrating on his swing, the caddie had taken the opportunity to remove the sword from the golf bag, raise it to a height level with the right ear of James, and swing it down hard at an angle of fifteen degrees from the horizontal, severing head from body in a single stroke. The caddie paused to admire his work alone because no others were able to see into the Z diagonal, and James himself, of course, was in no position to comment one way or the other. He then moved both parts of the body into the woods on the right-hand side, covering the blood stains on the grass itself with green chalk powder. He laid the headless body on its back, removed the stake from the golf bag, used a mallet to force it into the ground, and placed James's head on its top, slightly inclined as if looking down on his own body, then took a photograph. When the two players next in line located James in his severed condition an hour later both collapsed in shock, and they needed all the support they could get over the next few days to suppress what was for them a horrific sight. However, for many of the British public, who had suffered severely at the hands of financiers, the spectacle was to be evaluated rather differently.

The assassin now checked the time, opened his compass and headed east to the A 428, where he would meet his prearranged pick up who would transport him back to London. He looked forward to accessing the thirty thousand dollars to be deposited as soon as the death of James had been confirmed. Life was looking good; his rate of return per hour employed on this project matched that of his mark, and he, too, managed to convince himself that he had 'earned' every penny. The pickup had arrived two minutes before himself at the designated spot on the A 428, so he immediately opened the passenger door of the car, climbed in, and using the cell phone he found on the seat made the call before destroying the phone itself. He assumed that the official reporting of the death very soon would activate the money transfer and seal the fate of the James usual caddie. Of course, he did not know what would happen to him, but he did not much care either – he thought very much like a banker.

***

Stephanie Almiston was quite different from virtually all her banking colleagues. She was genuinely clever and regarded banking as a major threat to itself and all other industries. Moreover, she had grace, did not advertise her intelligence, and remained silent as to her views on modern finance. However, her opinions were very well founded. Despite originating from a lower middle-class background, she had in hand by the age of twenty-six a double first in philosophy and mathematics from the University of Oxford, a master's degree in statistics from MIT, and a Ph.D. in economics from the LSE. This expertise had been the foundation of her rapid rise to Vice President for Risk Management at Charter Investments Unlimited, a significantly large investment bank where she had begun to work ten years earlier. Her current salary was in the high six figures, matched by even larger bonuses, and had resulted in a fortune of over seventeen million pounds in investments, despite the fact that she took care of her family financially and invariably donated twenty percent of her income to charity. But Stephanie was under no illusions as to her achievements and would never have considered her remuneration as 'earnings'. Everything could be explained by her intelligence (which she recognized as a gift from God), luck (which probability theory explained insofar as it was explainable), and the incompetence of successive governments (which she considered to be but one prominent manifestation of the imperfection in all human institutions).

In her view, and it was very much an informed view, for the past forty-odd years governments had deregulated finance, proclaimed market incentives and mathematical modeling along with their own macroeconomic competence to be the key to systemic stability, and ignored all the empirical evidence to the contrary. Not that Stephanie actually needed to appeal to this evidence to support her views. Seen through the portals of Humean skepticism, or chaotic dynamics, or statistical theory, financial markets could easily become unstable. And the stability theorems of Walrasian general equilibrium analysis, let alone those of Keynes-Minsky economics, indicated capitalist economies were inherently volatile, and finance was the main propagation mechanism. But she had always remained silent. Prudence prevailed over authenticity, and the fact that she had been lucky with her risk modeling brought no personal crisis. Stephanie's bank had prospered where others had floundered, never really needing the liquidity offerings of the Bank of England or the bailouts of government largesse in the financial crises and in the Covid pandemic, but accepting of them only on the basis of what she considered to be the morals of the gutter.

Stephanie had in fact given evidence to several parliamentary inquiries into the crisis of 2008, along with the ensuing recession and stagnation in the British economy, and trotted out to perfection a standard line. The risk models of leading banks were robust; their managements were competent and responsible; regulators had for the most part done their jobs properly; capital requirements were not too low, and leverage had not been too high. She had also explained that the cause of the crisis lay in fraud, which was concentrated in America and had impacted on Britain analogous to an unforeseeable natural catastrophe. All this had been received with varied degrees of skepticism, but most of the MPs on the inquiries were ignoramuses when it came to finance, and Stephanie was not seriously challenged. Those MPs who did know something about banking were easily parried because they were allotted only their requisite share of time, which was rather short as the others wanted to say their set pieces before the cameras. The plan for her was to shift blame in much the same way if called to account for the recent financial crisis two months earlier.

Nonetheless, Stephanie had been bothered by her stand. She knew what she had said and would say was nonsense and in so doing had contributed to the guilty escaping judgment and the innocent suffering. The truth, of which she was well aware, was that most bankers did not understand the complex products created by 'financial engineers', not even the risk and compliance executives, let alone the regulators who were generally subpar. There was normally a considerable massaging of the numbers 'for the books', and complete hedging was impossible if only because of the regress – who could insure the insurers? Financial modeling was done on the basis of imperfect data over short periods of time exempt from any black-swan events. And even if it were accepted that the crisis had originated in America in 2008, and similarly so more recently, British financiers had failed to carry out their function of properly assessing the quality of the securities they purchased and the loans they made. Most people employed in banking did not work as hard as they pretended and were not as smart as they believed, but they most certainly received huge remunerations. These occurred as a result of the high profits that stemmed overwhelmingly from widespread fraud, monopoly power, informational advantages, and public subsidies. However, Stephanie had not even hinted at any of this in her past testimony and that which she planned for the future, instead playing the role assigned her as part of the structure and culture in which she worked and prospered.

However, a turning point had arrived in the form of Michelangelo, and on this bright sunny morning in late Spring her thoughts were centered on him once again. As with every other last Friday in the month, she began by walking to the station and taking the 10.15 a.m. train from Barnes into Waterloo terminal, then continuing along the South Bank, over the Millennium Bridge whilst admiring the beauty of Saint Paul's Cathedral and into her office eight minutes later. Wet or dry, it made no difference. The journey gave her an opportunity for exercise and to think on matters important, and these thoughts had increasingly come to focus on Michelangelo. They had met by chance when she had slipped on her way to work one morning several months earlier. Having momentarily lost consciousness, her first impressions on regaining it was that she was in the arms of Christ himself. Of course, reality reasserted itself, and she saw Michelangelo, who had gently lifted her from the concrete and now cradled her in his lap on a nearby seat. She was in all likelihood lost to him from this moment on, and the progression which followed seemed so natural; they had become friends, then lovers, and had then fallen in love. Of this Stephanie was certain. No such feelings of commitment, of unity, and of sacredness had ever infused her previous relationships. They had resulted only from the weakness of the flesh, but now that weakness was elevated to spiritual union. And since she believed the same held for Michelangelo, a new life became possible: an ethical life, a life of meaning, and a life closer to God, all of which necessarily meant a life outside of finance.

Michelangelo, like his namesake, was a sculptor and painter who had traveled to London to study the superb collections in the many museums. He had no money to speak of and stayed in some seedy bed-and-breakfast in Brixton, but he was a truly beautiful man in all the ways that mattered to her. She knew he was becoming anxious to return to Tuscany and remained in England only because she was there, so the thought had begun to mature in her mind of them going to Italy together, purchasing a villa near Florence, and perhaps even beginning a family. He could continue with his art; she could begin a new intellectual and spiritual path. There were no significant impediments to doing so, certainly not financial ones.

But it was not to be. A transformation would come, but not the one she anticipated. It was too late. Stephanie's record of compliance and silence in the sins of modern banking had condemned her. She was to be the fourth assassinated. But it had been a difficult decision for The Committee. They recognized that this killing had a tragic quality. Modern finance had not just incorporated fraudsters, sociopaths and spivs; it had corrupted the very best. This truth had to be conveyed and in picking their targets they were in deadly seriousness that this message would be received.

As Stephanie approached the end of the lane that wound its way behind the houses close to the Barnes station, a woman in a flowing cape and large hat approached from the opposite direction. After they had passed each other, the woman turned, raised her right arm inside the cape and fired a single shot into the left-hand side of Stephanie's back with a silenced Glock .4 pistol, smashing her heart and killing her instantly. There were no apparent witnesses but had there been it would have appeared to most of them that Stephanie had stumbled, perhaps fainted, and it would have taken several minutes for them to provide any assistance. The woman in the cape continued walking rapidly, passed Stephanie once again, exited the lane, continued toward the station and opened the door of a nearby car. A phone lay on the adjacent seat, the call was placed, the phone destroyed, and the money transfer would follow.

*** 

Billy Jones, owner of Super Comp Trading (SCT), was unusual, although in a hugely different way from Stephanie Almiston. He was a product of the lower ranks of the working class, Bolton Comprehensive High School and Salford University. This was far from the pedigree associated with anyone in the City, at least for those much higher than a clerk. However, Billy had often been astute; he had taken a degree in computing in the late 1990s, found he had a real facility with the machines, and when an otherwise 'family-free' distant relative had died in Australia who left his mother nearly two million pounds he persuaded her to let him use half to set up his company. That was fifteen years ago, and he now had an annual income of around ten million pounds, and wealth of sixty million. As his mother used to say to her old friends, "Hasn't Billy done well," and there was no demurring that she was right. It was certainly a surprise to one and all, and not just because of his social origins. He was also an ugly and unpleasant child, and everyone bar his mother wished him only the worst.

SCT specialized in high-frequency trading, using suitably programmed mainframe computers to enact trades at lightning speed. Profits came from buying information from companies providing data services minutes, sometimes seconds, before the release to most other customers. The data was machine readable and fed directly to the computers, which then enacted trades according to the algorithms with which they were programmed. This allowed gains to be realized from an information advantage, and although in this case it was not illegal, like many other informational advantages possessed by finance firms it had no social value but was highly profitable. Likewise, with the second major activity, which involved the computers placing buy and sell orders in ways that were designed to reveal the trading algorithms of others, and then take profitable advantage of this information at the cost of these traders. SCT was also located as close as possible to the exchanges on which trades were enacted, gaining a mille second advantage on trading in publicly available information. All three activities had been crucial in the crisis of 2008 and in the more recent one two months earlier, as well as in the turbulence induced by the Covid 19 outbreak. The firm had made a small fortune in all cases, while others had gone belly-up in part because of their losses to SCT. However, none of this came cheap, whether with market turbulence or stability. The company had a small staff of geeks and quants, but they were paid handsomely, the computer hardware was extremely costly, and the rents were sky-high.

Billy was also innovative in matters of which he had only minimal understanding. He had used the services of one of the big accounting companies, Anderton Partners and Associates, to do what was necessary in registering the company in Guernsey and thereby take advantage of this tax haven status. He had assurances that this was perfectly legal so far as the letter of the law was concerned, and for Billy as well as his accountants this was enough. As he sometimes said, "The spirit of the law should be shoved where the sun don't shine." But it was not that Billy's vulgarity was concerned only with making money. Far from it, he wanted status, and status of the old-fashioned sort, by becoming 'the top of the heap' in what he imagined would be the cozy warmth of a local community. As any reputable sociologist might have told him, this was impossible to attain in the modern world, but he had a blind spot when it came to stratification theory and assumed money suitably spent could buy anything. As a result, Billy had purchased two 'assets', a country estate in Wiltshire and a wife of the 'right' 'origins' and 'skill set' who had fallen on hard times financially. Both were attractive, and so far as Cecily was concerned an unexpected bonus had occurred. She seemed to have developed some genuine affection for him after their marriage two years earlier, and he had become wholly entranced by her, even though she still absolutely refused to be referred to as Mrs. Jones and strongly recommended he change his own name by deed poll.

He began to think about this after she persuaded him that it was a necessary, albeit not sufficient, condition for success in his plan of rising in the social scale. Achievement here would be satisfying enough, but Billy also dreamed sometimes of leveraging it to attain entry into even higher circles, perhaps even the aristocracy. He had confided all this one day to one of his quants of German origin who subsequently had coined the nickname "Volks-Gemeinschaft Billy". When Billy himself had first heard this by accident and had the Deutsch translated to him, he lost his temper and produced a mouthful of invective directed at German notions of the master race, immediately firing the quant in question, followed by aggression that bordered on serious violence. So, most people in the City who knew Billy played safe and never mentioned either origins or social ambitions, merely assuming that he had not managed to fully cast off all the limitations they associated with anyone born in the 'Deep North'.

This Friday he was driving from London to his country estate to ensure that all was going to be perfect with the party which he and Cecily were giving that evening. All the really important people of the county had been invited and no expense had been spared, including the purchase of seventy bottles of 2024 Dom Perignon, an equal number of Lafitte Rothschild 99, twenty-five lb. of smoked Scottish salmon, forty-five lb. of the finest Alberta beef, a large amount of the freshest home-produced vegetables and fruits, along with a team of chefs from London to cook and serve. It promised to be a great success, but he was leaving nothing to chance. He was now in his Porsche X5 on the B4596 heading into Wiltshire. This was not a direct route to his estate, Haversharm, but it was the most enjoyable. Relatively unused, with long straight sections and good visibility on a sunny day, it easily allowed safe and rapid accelerations with extraordinarily little chance of being caught for speeding. Billy had seen the helicopter proceeding in the same direction, but he took no notice of it. He had no reason to do so because it was not a police machine as he had recognized it as one from the local rental company. Moreover, he was unaware of the Semtex explosives that had been attached to the Porsche while in the garage the preceding night.

The Committee's instructions had been clear and precise, as it had been with the other four assassinations preceding it. Billy was to be eliminated, but there was to be no collateral damage in the form of other deaths or excessive damage to property. If the contract could not be completed in this way, it was to be aborted. Another assassination would be activated in its stead.

Today, the two men in the helicopter had no anxiety: the weather was fine, the road was clear in both directions for several miles, no houses or animals were in the vicinity, and the car was about to approach the first long straight section. Five seconds after Billy had pressed down hard on the accelerator the passenger in the helicopter pressed down gently on the detonator. As Billy would have known, such signals travel at close to the speed of light, and the Porsche was lifted thirty feet into the air and transformed into a huge fireball. Job completed, the helicopter veered away to return to base, the call was made, the phone destroyed, and the financial transfer would follow. However, the man in the passenger seat of the helicopter was not overly pleased with the result, remarking later that the explosion was much larger than he had calculated. His companion smiled and responded, "The car must have had fuel tanks retrofitted, but there is no need to be worry as the contract was carried out impeccably, and the fireworks had been nothing short of a sendoff fit for a Lord."

The designated member of The Committee received the fifth communication and immediately ordered the other assassins to stand down, as these would have proceeded only if any of the first five had failed. The second stage of the plan was then initiated – presenting a list of demands for action by the British government.

# II REACTION

Immediately upon The Committee receiving confirmation of the satisfactory completion of the five killings by the assassins who had carried them out, all the major British media outlets operating through print, radio, television, and the internet received the following statement of purpose. It was subsequently made public after their preliminary checks had indicated that, while it might be exaggerated and deluded, it was not likely to be a hoax and was obviously important.

*Statement of Purpose. Today, The Committee of National Rejuvenation carried out five acts designed to realign British politics and society behind a different set of priorities than those which presently prevail. The acts themselves were violent, but our intentions and objectives are quite the reverse. We seek a unified country, where conciliation of different interests can form a consensus as a result of those holding leading positions playing their roles appropriately, recognizing their duties as well as receiving their rewards, so allowing the nation to be re-established as a more unified, prosperous and secure entity.*

*Between 9.00 a.m. and 10.30 a.m. five bankers were assassinated. In many ways, they were quite different from each other, but all played a significant part in the activities of companies which brought on the financial crisis of 2008 or that of two months ago, as well as the ensuing economic stagnation. They had, therefore, contributed to the immiseration of many millions of lives, and the dashing of the legitimate hopes of millions more. What they and others in finance had done should not be forgotten or forgiven and for the selected five the forgiv-*

ing stopped this morning. However, from a broader perspective, they themselves were but representatives of larger forces that have subverted the politics, the economy and the society of Britain for many decades, and we regard their deaths as a means through which rejuvenation can begin. The restraints required to maintain social functionality and harmony between the individuals and groups that comprise our nation have been seriously weakened, and a culture of unrestrained greed and sharp practices has strengthened, allowing a flowering of individual licence and of divisions that have brought a fraying of communal connections and responsibilities. Policies over successive governments have contributed significantly to this awful situation, and there needs to be a program of widespread and significant change implemented.

No doubt, our actions will be condemned as terrorist, but there is no need to debate this designation because we are more than willing to plead guilty. The acts are meant to terrorize those who have undermined the virtues that we value and have the power to set another course. But it is only those that need to feel threatened, and the higher circles of British society must take special note of this in order to begin the task of repair. In furtherance of this task, we guarantee no further assassinations will occur for at least one month. Consequently, there is no need for panic, and there is an opportunity for public support to be shown for the policies we propose, as well as time for those with power to begin implementing them and reestablish the nation as it should be.

The objectives we seek are of the highest importance and accord with what the majority of British people believe to be appropriate: the creation of a prosperous, orderly and decent society that spreads through the whole of the land, ruled by a sovereign parliament that is genuinely representative of all the principal interests constituting the nation, and where all recognize their duty to act responsibly rather than opportunistically. This is not the present reality. Stated in compressed form, *the truth is that Britain has an economy centred on London, an abused and fractious society, and a deluded political class. The City is at the center of the rot, using its immense power to ensure government policies favour it so skewing the structure of economic activity to the South of the country. Moreover, the heart of this activity focusses on extractive activities on a global scale in which every form of sharp practice is employed. In particular, the parasitism includes draining resources out of Britain itself, rather than promoting the productive activities of the country as a whole. Moreover, this structure of exploitation is unsustainable, as evidenced by the recent financial crisis and its predecessor in 2008. These did not result from an unpredictable black-swan event, but from the irresponsible actions of financial executives and the institutions they control, which have been empowered by successive governments to act in their own selfish interests and have not been aligned with those of the nation.*

*Redemption lies along a clear path: ensuring all elites recognize that they have social obligations and duties as well as personal ambitions, so bringing a social stability that can coexist with individual freedoms. Thus, there is a need to begin by subordinating finance to national needs, focusing it on supporting genuinely productive activity, and eliminating its present fraudulent and exploitative orientations, as well as strengthening institutions of civil society, along with those of the family and local communities.*

*Our intervention today represents but five warning shots as to what will happen on a much larger scale if the political class continues along its present path. Obviously, it would be prudent for the government to act positively in the ways we suggest, and in an endeavour to promote this more rational solution we request that the British public demonstrate their support for our actions and our recommendations in all ways appropriate to doing so.*

***

Just before the Prime Minister was informed of the assassinations, he was in an intense discussion with the American Secretary of State who was seeking to persuade him to commit British troops in support of a planned invasion of Iran. As the Secretary himself put the issue, "for the purpose of supporting freedom and democracy and finally beginning to establish a civilized Middle East." Like all prime ministers since the end of the Second World War, Johnathan Easton believed there to be a need to subordinate Britain to the power of America and was desperate to keep Britain in a special relationship that was markedly fraying. However, while he was willing to venture yet another mission in 'the region', he knew that Parliament would not support his government in doing so. Indeed, some within the government would not, and it would be most unlikely to get a majority in his own parliamentary party. Thus, he was snookered and was trying to explain this to the Secretary, who seemed unaware of the nature of "freedom and democracy" in Britain itself, and who thought he was being palmed off with little more than lame excuses. But, in a sense he was right, at least partially. While the excuses might not be lame, they were excuses. The British government had the authority to act militarily without the support of the House of Commons. However, it did not have the capacity to win a confidence vote in the event of doing so, and if there was one thing that Johnathan Easton thought more important than "freedom and democracy" in the Middle East or even remaining in the good books of the United States, it was that he should remain Prime Minister in Britain.

Fortunately, or as it would turn out unfortunately, the Cabinet Secretary, Sir Richard Armitage, interrupted the meeting and requested the Prime Minister's full attention in order to attend to a matter of the "utmost urgency". Apologies were made to the Secretary, who was quickly ushered out of the Prime Minister's office and transported back to the American Embassy along with his large retinue of guards. As soon as he was out of the room, Sir Richard outlined the events that were so far known. He spoke slowly and deliberately, "There appear to have been three assassinations in London and vicinity, and perhaps one more, as well as a highly suspicious explosion in Wiltshire. Three people, all connected with the City, were killed earlier this morning in a markedly professional manner and sometimes in gruesome ways. Rory Candiman was garrotted, and James Stewart was decapitated, and Stephanie Almiston was shot." Ignoring the fact that the Prime minister had stood up and gone very pale, the Cabinet Secretary continued, "Moreover, the car of Sir Roger Gilchrest has been found on the B2212 about twenty miles south-west of central London, and the emergency services are still attempting to gain entry, which is proving very, very difficult. It is suspected that he will have been killed too. And in Wiltshire there has been a huge explosion near the Haversharm estate which is owned by a William Jones, who operates a hedge fund in the City, and who was due to arrive at his country home over an hour ago but has not done so." Sir Richard then handed the Prime Minister two sheets of paper containing the Committee's demands, simultaneously advising him to take a seat while he read it.

This was a wise piece of advice. Unlike Sir Richard, the Prime Minister tended to panic. Naturally, he was far from stupid and was popular with his own faction in the party, which lay on the market-promoting right. But he also knew he had been lucky to get the leadership, win the last election and so far at least successfully manage dissent in parliament. The tension and stress made him look considerably older than his forty-four years, even though he was careful to remain attractive in appearance, was always smartly dressed, well-spoken, and usually gave off an air of confidence. So, the impact on Jonathan Easton of reading The Committee's statement was one of severe shock increasingly followed by horror and then an element of fear. In this case though he kept his composure and simple asked, "What do you think this means?"

To which Sir Richard responded rather gravely, "That remains to be determined sir. I suggest we convene a COBRA meeting as soon as possible, with all the relevant ministers, security service personnel and officers of the metropolitan police present. We probably cannot do this for several hours, but by then we should have a much clearer picture of exactly what is afoot. The police are undertaking all that can be done to find the perpetrators of these crimes, and I have every confidence in their abilities."

The Prime Minister interjected, "This looks more like a matter of national security and if MI5 and MI6 could be trusted, it would have been nipped in the bud before anyone was killed. They can hardly claim that budget cuts have incapacitated them like other government departments because they have had huge increases in their funds every year for well over a decade. You know this as well as I do. Sir Roger Gilchrest was, and hopefully still *is*, a close friend of both the Chancellor and I, a talented banker and fine human being, which Britain can ill afford to lose *if lost he is*. I want no shilly-shalling on this matter. Get Sir Roger's car opened as soon as possible and have armed guards assigned to all leading bankers if they are presently without protection. God alone knows what this will do the City. I need not tell you that I am exceedingly worried."

Sir Richard was unfazed. He had a long experience in dealing with ministers and prime ministers of both parties and did not rate their abilities at all highly, let alone most of their policies. On his second reading of the Committee's statement, he recognized a twinge of sympathy for the path there recommended. However, he was too much of a professional to linger on these thoughts or question his duty and agreed with the Prime Minister on this occasion that this could prove to be a major crisis. Thus, it had to be countered with the full spectrum of the powers available to the state. His deepest fear was that this was a more targeted version of 9/11, equally focused on one of the pillars of Western economic power and even more professional in execution, but he doubted that this was actually the case in the light of the Committee's statement. As he left the room, he said to the Prime Minister, "Yes, it could be a dire situation in many ways. I will convene the COBRA meeting for later today."

***

Just after 6.00 p.m., the Prime Minister, Cabinet Secretary, several senior ministers of the government, a few civil servants, heads of the two principal security services, MI5 and MI6, along with the Commissioner of the Metropolitan police, gathered in Cabinet Office Briefing Room A (COBRA). It was not an especially large meeting, but secure video links had also been established with other personnel, including officers in several regional police forces. The Prime Minister opened the meeting by asking everyone to introduce themselves, and then immediately requested the Cabinet Secretary for an update of events. He began with information on the assassinations, "You will all have read the statement from those who have claimed responsibility for the five assassinations this morning. At the time of its release we had confirmation of three killings: those of Rory Candiman, James Stewart and Stephanie Almiston, and somewhat later the deaths of Sir Roger Gilchrest and William Jones. The car of Sir Roger was eventually opened by the emergency services, and forensic scientists have matched fragments from the explosion in Wiltshire with William Jones body and car. All these five people were connected to the City and professionally executed in multiple ways. Those claiming responsibility have made a set of demands on the government for a substantial change in government policy and promise no further actions for at least a month. Assuming they keep their word, we, therefore, have a period of time to locate and either apprehend or destroy them. The investigation is currently being headed by MI5, but they are coordinating with the other security services and police forces. Sir Crispin Prendergaton, the Head of 5, will update us on progress so far when called upon to do so."

The Prime Minister thanked Sir Richard and immediately turned to Sir Crispin requesting his own update on the investigation. He, too, began with the assassinations, "All five killings were carried out with an exceedingly high degree of professionalism and in multiple ways indicating considerable organizational and technical capabilities. So, there should be no misunderstanding that this is a formidable enemy. However, our own capabilities should also not be underestimated. We have already begun to examine all the CCTV footage available, although the focused footage is quite slim because of the location of the killings. And all electronic communications thought to be relevant are under examination by Government Communications Headquarters (GCHQ). We have also had the police undertake a search for witnesses, and this is also ongoing, as well as the interviewing of people that had recently come in contact with the five victims. Our principal goal, of course, is to determine what terrorist group is responsible. But there are a large set of possibilities – various cells of jihadists, the IRA, foreign intelligence services of hostile powers, as well as organized crime syndicates. Investigations are continuing, and we are coordinating intimately with MI6 and foreign intelligence services in countries of our closest allies."

Jonathan Easton neglected to thank the head of MI5 and immediately responded, "From what you say, I take it that you haven't a bloody clue who did this and not much evidence that will bring a determination in the near future." Holding his hand up to preclude a response, the Prime Minister continued, "I cannot stress how important it is to find these people quickly. The City is in uproar and could be severely damaged if there is not a speedy end to this matter, and any delay resulting from inefficiency would reverse all the hard work accomplished with our efforts to increase business confidence. Moreover, there could be more strikes against other important groups of people, which would completely destroy the economic recovery. I think the damage that could be done as analogous to a major invasion. I am not exaggerating. The City represents the very finest economic institutions and personnel we have and what they do constitutes the life blood of the nation. Sir Roger Gilchrest was a personal friend of mine and will be sadly missed. I want the bastards who did this caught, and I want them caught quickly. In order to facilitate this, I propose that we declare a state of emergency immediately and use all the powers thereby made available to secure a result sooner rather than later. And you should also know Sir Crispin that Her Majesty's Government is awfully close to losing all confidence and trust in MI5 and MI6."

With that the Prime Minister opened up the meeting for discussion, and the Foreign Secretary, Michael Madlen, was the first to speak, "Yes, the Prime Minister is absolutely correct on all counts. This is not a normal emergency or even a normal terrorist attack. It is a strike at the heart of Britain, and all powers necessary for the expeditious resolution to the crisis must be employed."

"Thank you, Michael," responded the Prime Minister, "Does anyone want to add anything?"

This was the cue the Home Secretary, John Johnston, who was increasingly regarded as a rival to the Prime Minister, was waiting for, and he intervened with a contrary view, " I agree that this is an unusually dangerous attack, but I want to stress even more than has already been done that those responsible are also likely to be exceptionally skilled and are unlikely to be brought to book quickly unless we are particularly lucky. Moreover, I think declaring a state of emergency is wrong-headed and likely counterproductive. Whether we approve or not, what the Committee says about the City and the need for alternative public policies has a large degree of popular support and not only in the country outside of London. No doubt, the fitful nature of the economic recovery keeps the financial crisis and hostility to bankers in the public's consciousness. Nonetheless, when that is coupled to the powers available under a state of emergency, which in effect is a suspension of the law of the land, I fear that some incident or set of incidents could generate a social explosion. So far, the population has been relatively quiescent in the face of the financial crisis, and the damage caused by the bankers, and that may change if some of them begin to meet the heavy hand of state power. We should stay cool and collected and prepare for the present situation to continue for some time. We certainly should not overreact."

The Prime Minister could barely contain himself in the face of such a frontal assault on his own policies. This had been going on for some time and were it not for the fact that the Home Secretary had substantial support in the parliamentary party, he would have been replaced months ago. Moreover, the Prime Minister strongly suspected that John Johnston harbored sympathies for the changes that The Committee sought to impose. He had continually critiqued the policies of the government, which he referred to as "featherbedding the City," and wanted a much more stringent set of measures that he said would "re-establish the national economy on a stronger and more equitable basis." In the Prime Minister's judgment, the present attack came close to treason and certainly had to be forcefully rebutted, so he called on others to "make their own contribution."

However, little of substance was said, but it was usually said at great length. Virtually everyone who spoke supported the Prime Minister, although Jonathan Easton believed he detected a less than enthusiastic endorsement among some of his ministers. "No doubt hedging their bets," he thought to himself. Nonetheless, what was said was enough for the Prime Minister to call for an end of discussion at around 7.15 p.m. and summarize the consensus of the meeting. He spoke slowly and deliberately, "Thank you ladies and gentlemen; I think we are at a juncture where it is eminently clear what the general will is. We must use all our resources to apprehend the terrorists quickly, and the powers inherent in the declaration of a state of emergency will contribute positively to this goal. I will sign the requisite authorizations immediately on returning to Number 10, and this will be broadcast to the country through all major channels immediately. COBRA will, of course, meet as required, but hopefully the crisis that brought us together today will soon be over." With that he closed the meeting. However, before leaving the Cabinet Secretary took the Commissioner of the Metropolitan Police to one side and requested him to meet with the Prime Minister at Number 10 immediately.

***

It took only a few minutes for the Prime Minister to return to his main office in Downing Street, and only a little longer for him to begin his meeting with the Commissioner of the Metropolitan Police, Alexander Hendry, who was to say the least rather puzzled as to why he had been singled out. But the Prime Minister quickly put him at ease by explaining that he wanted a change in what the head of MI5 thought to be the usual responsibilities for the investigation into the murder of the five bankers, and the threats subsequently posted. "Alex, you already know that my reservations about MI5 have been deepening for some time, and I understand that both you and the Cabinet Secretary have similar concerns, so I want to shift responsibility for the present investigation elsewhere. Special Branch under your jurisdiction has very competent officers and cooperative and productive relations with people in the other services, as well as other sections of the Met and regional police forces, so I want them to head the investigation. Of course, they will coordinate with  all other departments of state, but I want Special Branch in charge, and I want the best Commander you have to lead the investigation, and I want to meet him as soon as I can to impress on him myself that I regard this matter as no less than existential for the Defence of the Realm."

The Commissioner knew better than try to qualify anything the Prime Minister had said and, indeed, had no incentive to do so. He had come off badly when he had previously sought to advise the Prime Minister without prior invitation to offer an opinion and had no intention of repeating the mistake. Moreover, the Commissioner was also always eager to increase the prominence of the Met in any way possible. His response was, therefore, not drawn out, "Of course, Prime Minister, I have exactly the right man in mind and will have him here to meet you within the hour. He is exceptionally able." With that the Commissioner was ushered out by the Cabinet Secretary and immediately placed a call to Commander Charles Ryder at Scotland Yard, requesting his presence at Number 10 as soon as possible. He then waited in the ante room for Ryder to arrive and got ready to brief him on the Prime Minister's reallocation of responsibilities before another meeting with the Prime Minister himself.

It took less than thirty minutes for Commander Ryder to appear. The Commissioner stood up and shook his hand, thanking him for his promptness. He then spent several minutes apprising him of the Prime Minister's intentions and asking whether he had any reservations in having command and responsibility of the overall investigation. Since Charles Ryder was highly intelligent, confident and competent, he had already worked out that something important was in the offing, and that the events of the day would be at the centre of the matter, so he had factored in what possibilities might be afoot. He allayed any fears that the Commissioner could have and assured him that he himself and Special Branch were up to the task of leading the investigation and coordinating the specialists of all the other organizations if need be. Indeed, he said, the Branch had already begun contributing to investigations of the killings, and it would not be difficult to take on the leading role. At the same time, he candidly expressed his belief that it would not be an easy task to bring the perpetrators to justice. Like everyone else, he had been struck by the disciplined qualities so evident in the assassinations and, like many others, also with the qualities of the analysis, and the demands they had made in their Statement of Purpose, which he had already read several times. The Commissioner said nothing, but by his nodding indicated that he too had arrived at similar conclusions. However, he did explicitly warn the Commander not to be too negative with the Prime Minister.

When Jonathan Easton met him twenty minutes later, he could not help in being surprised at the Commander's relative youth (he was in fact thirty-eight, but looked five years younger), good looks and self-assurance, yet without any hint of arrogance. Nature and nurture had certainly been kind to Charles Ryder. He was six-foot-tall with excellent posture, a handsome face, always stylish in dress and typically popular with colleagues at the Yard. The Prime Minister took to the Commander immediately, checked that he had been briefed by the Commissioner and then added some further comments, "If you meet any problems that resist solution through the normal channels, you may contact me directly and at any time of the day or night. The same applies to the Cabinet Secretary in the event of my absence or if I am indisposed by other business. And I want to emphasize that you may do whatever is necessary to solve these crimes. However unconventional necessary turns out to be, I will support you one hundred percent. You have my word on this. After we part, the Cabinet Secretary will provide you with the relevant contact numbers which are fully secure. I would also stress that you should feel no hesitation in using to the full powers conferred by the declaration of a state of emergency. These supplement those powers already available under the anti-terrorism laws. Obviously, they may be useful to you in all manner of ways, but, in addition, I take the view that what the organizers of the killings propose as an alternative to the policies of my government is highly popular with a small minority in this country, and they will need treating appropriately by the police and all other agencies of the state if they show support for the assassinations." With that the Prime Minister shook the Commander's hand again, wished him well in the investigation, and ended their meeting.

***

The Prime Minister's belief that the events of the day would prove popular with a "small minority" was wrong in both respects; there was no indication that it was a minority at all, and, if it was, it was far from small. Many people were vocal and spirited from the beginning. Much later, commentators who looked back on the events of the first weekend after the assassinations would describe them as the beginning of the 'great awakening'. This description was indeed appropriate. Britain had experienced the 2008 financial crisis followed by economic downturn, and then austerity for many years followed by yet another financial crisis only two months earlier, but the populace had remained overwhelmingly passive. There had, of course, been Brexit activities, which could be described as excited, but they had not been targeted at the economically privileged in finance and related activities. Likewise, the disruptions of Covid 19 had been widespread, but here had been no focus of hostility on the rich and powerful. Now this began to change, and there were six episodes that commentators pointed to as emblematic in showing the extent to which the Committee's actions garnered widespread approval so quickly.

The first began the very evening of the assassinations. Like that of every Friday, the pubs in and around the City were full of junior bankers, and the large contingent of young women who sought to attract and attach themselves to bankers. That, of course, was why many of the men who worked in the City were in the pubs in the first place. Perhaps this was surprising, but most pub goers seemed to have taken the Committee at its word that there would be no more killings immediately. What was new on the evening of the assassinations, though, were the other visitors to the area who were less attractive and sought to attach themselves to bankers in a rather different manner. They too had come to join in the 'conversation' about the events of the day and were beginning such with shouts and jeers rejoicing in the carnage. Naturally, the language was not overly sophisticated, but it was not expressed ambiguously, usually beginning with something of the form, "We got five of you bastards today, and that's just for beginners".

Another chant was, "We popped five today, and there will be fifty tomorrow and five hundred on Sunday", which, of course, could be faulted as The Committee was unlikely to have included these yobs in its deliberations and decision making, and because it took no account of the pledge given by the Committee itself to cease assassinations for a month.

However, in the circumstances then prevailing, it was not the logic to which the bankers took principal exception. And since many of them had had too much to drink, and quite a few had training in the martial arts, their response was very physical. Fights broke out everywhere, but typically it was the bankers that came off worse. After all, the intruders into the City had come from the poorer areas of London where street fighting skills had been absorbed not long after their mothers' milk. In contrast, the Karate, Tai Kwon Do, Aikido, and suchlike skills of the bankers proved pretty useless as all had been learnt by punching and kicking into space during set drills in air conditioned gyms, following traditions many centuries in the making and considerably at variance with the type of agro required to survive fighting in the modern city. They had never even imagined that street fighting regularly involved weaponizing the local environment, such as slamming heads against walls, along with head butts to the groin, biting noses and gouging the eyes, but they were treated to such experiences in great abundance this evening. The police were not long in arriving on the scene, but they were way outnumbered initially, and themselves came off rather badly too. Reinforcements arrived in due course and ended the disorders, mainly by chasing off the interlopers; although, a few arrests were also made. The police had an instinctual reaction to side with the bankers and had no difficulty in distinguishing the combatants. After all, it was only the bankers who were dressed as gentlemen, and none of the women fighting were without extensive tattoos, or spiked hair and piercings.

The following Saturday morning there was another notable incident originating from a rather different class of people and in the most unusual of places, the School of the Royal Ballet. There had been a new curriculum introduced some years earlier that devoted Saturday morning classes to the study of management and entrepreneurship. It was felt by the governing board that the lack of popularity of the dance form lay not in its refinement, but in its marketing. After much discussion with a multitude of business consultants, it was concluded that the appropriate path was to promote 'innovative ways of thinking' (the phrase was used routinely) among the students. Thus, the students that morning were in the fourth week of the sessions on 'Innovation and Entrepreneurship'. But this session was to be quite different. At the beginning of the class one of the ballerinas raised her hand and posed the question of whether or not the assassination of five bankers yesterday was an entrepreneurial strategy well designed to promote innovation in public policy and what impact might it have on rejuvenating ballet.

As it happened, the session that morning was devoted to the topic of raising capital and corporate finance and was being taught by one of the banking community. He did not take the question at all well and proceeded to launch into a defence of all things financial, sweating profusely in the process. When he appeared to have finished, another student asked whether the class could take his answer to be negative, or at least negatively inclined as it had not actually seemed to have been explicit. The poor man was by now quite beside himself and hurriedly left the room to the sound of the jeers of the students. They, too, then left soon afterwards and walked as a group toward Covent Garden where they began to shout, "Bugger business! Blast the bankers!" which despite its lack of rhythmical quality attracted a large chorus of people in the square. While this was certainly making the ballet dancers more popular, and thus, perhaps, contributing to achieving the goals of their studies earlier that morning, the local constabulary failed to make the connection. Not that they were required to do so as there was a state of emergency in place, and their orders were, literally, the only law left. Perhaps remembering the experience of some of their colleagues the previous evening, batons were drawn and used causing considerable injury to students and public alike. Unlike the interlopers of the previous evening, they were considerably less skilled in using their mouths, feet, knees, fists, elbows, head, and the immediate environment to defend themselves. But as it happened, some of the yobs from the conflict of the previous evening in the City were also in the neighbourhood and were able to offer considerable assistance to the students by employing their own skill set in defence.The acts of courage shown became legendary and would never be forgotten. So, a peculiar solidarity began.

The third 'incident' attaining iconic status was in the early evening of Saturday at a lecture by Lord Duffort, who had been relatively unknown to most of the British public until a few months before. Then, there had been an *expose* in one of the main politics magazines of his pivotal role in the British participation of the invasion of Iraq, and this had been picked up by many of the newspapers and widely broadcast. It was thus now common knowledge that he had been one of the principal links between the British and American governments and had participated in the misleading of the former, so ensuring their compliance with the delusions of the latter about the possible democratization of the Middle East and the existence of weapons of mass destruction in Iraq. He was, therefore, very much 'damaged goods' in the eyes of a large section of the nation and now never appeared anywhere without a large retinue of protection. It was because of this security, and because he wanted to change the topic from a defence of his foreign policy achievements to 'speak to the people' about the domestic events of the previous day that he had not cancelled the engagement. He began soberly, calling for the families of the victims to be remembered in peoples' prayers, and then went on to demand an uncompromising reaction against this attack on eminent figures in the leading institutions of the country.

At this very point, about twenty men stood up from their seats in the aisles and moved quickly to the platform where Duffort was holding forth. Neither he, nor his protectors, seemed to notice for a second or two, but later people in the very front row did recount seeing his expression change quite markedly thereafter; although, he could not have known at the time quite how pathetic his bodyguards would prove to be. As it subsequently transpired, the men were not of the 'general public' but battle-hardened former paratroopers who had fought in Iraq, in some cases on multiple tours. The pointlessness of all the violence was only too evident to them, and they regarded what they were about to do as a tribute to their many fallen comrades. It had, in fact, been planned for over a month, and the events of the previous day had only increased the resolve to execute it to perfection. Most of the paras devoted themselves to immobilizing the defences attempted by the bodyguards, while another five grabbed Duffort, one at each limb and one at the head. They were not very gentle with him, but physical harm was not the priority in their agenda on this occasion. Instead, it was to be humiliation of a tar-and-feathering variety that was their plan. Tar was obviously not available, so treacle was substituted and poured liberally over the Lord's now bared body. Bags of feathers were then emptied and patted quite roughly into place. Duffort was returned to his feet, which had been handcuffed together, as were his wrists behind his back, so he was immobilized and left on view for the remainder of the audience, some of whom were clapping and shouting their support. The newspapers of the next morning all had photographs of one of the former prime movers of catastrophe in Iraq, both as he entered the hall to speak and as he was shortly after his speaking had been cut short. Sales were particularly good that Sunday.

The fourth event commentators generally considered representative of the 'great awakening' was similar to the Duffort episode in many respects. It had been under discussion for some time, but in this case, there were many conspirators who lacked the resolve to carry out the plans. It had, therefore, become bogged down into a lot of politicking between radicals (as they were known) and constitutionalists (as they were also known). However, the Committee's dramatic actions and statement of purpose had the effect of turning a large number of constitutionalists into radicals and plans for the Sunday morning were quickly activated. The target was Bertram Pickle and his guests as they were having a sumptuous Sunday brunch at his country home in the Wye valley. Branston, as he was often called, had purchased it several years earlier and was now engaged in using his extensive battery of lawyers to undermine the traditional rights of passage across his considerable lands. This was much to the detriment of the South Eastern Wales Rambling Association, and the members were determined to resist in one way or another.

The weather was very accommodating, with a mid-morning temperature around eighteen degrees, beautiful blue skies and light winds. This, of course, was very suitable for the brunch to be an especially enjoyable affair. But the fine weather was to be a great boon to the ramblers too. One of their number worked in a facility that disposed of food passed its 'best before date' and was able to divert about one hundred and fifty dozen eggs into the hands of the forty-three ramblers who committed to the operation. Since they knew the territory very well, they were able to approach the rear lawn where brunch was taking place unnoticed through the woods that edged the lawn on three sides, with the house itself forming the fourth edge. At 11.20 a.m., with Branston's twenty odd guests well tucked into their smoked salmon and sipping champagne, the ramblers made their move. Like a well-drilled regiment, they emerged from their hiding places and loosed their ordinance. Since the range was short, many of the ramblers young, fit, and with excellent eyesight, they had little difficulty hitting their targets. Moreover, because the number of eggs far exceeded the number of the guests and their host, most were struck multiple times before they managed to retreat indoors, especially as the ramblers closer to the house itself were larger in number than their colleagues at the bottom of the lawn. Branston himself took rather more hits than the average, not as a result of any valour on his part in defending others, but because he was such a striking and hated figure, he attracted more projectiles than his fair share. It had been well planned and even better executed, with most people judging that the eggs had really not been appropriately classified as beyond their 'best before date' earlier than that Sunday.

The fifth incident came from an entirely different location in the social spectrum, quite distinct from yobs, ballerinas, former armed services personnel, and ramblers. The Sunday Chronicle newspaper, popular with all classes of reader, had included an interview with Philip Stapleton, head of the Association of UK Manufacturers (AUKM) and an eminent industrialist himself. While it had been scheduled long before, being undertaken on the Saturday, it not unnaturally focused on the events of the preceding

Friday, and the Committee's statement was a central topic. Indeed, the interviewee demanded it be so, and the interviewer had no objection as the topic was "very hot".

Naturally, Phillip Stapleton went through the conventional motions of condemning the violence, but it was noticeable that he did not dwell on the matter and used only standard clichés. He was much more concerned to stress that the statement of The Committee had pointed to genuine and long-standing problems in Britain, which he believed had an economic cause he could shed much light on. In particular, they reflected the fact that since the 1980s Britain had adopted an "industrial policy for finance" rather than a "financial policy for industry". Thus, everything had become topsy-turvy, and the damage inflicted on the British economy and British society had been huge. Using its enhanced power, the City had promoted globalization rather than national production, ensuring that domestic manufacturing shrank dramatically. Today, it constituted less than ten percent of economic activity in the country – a truly shocking contraction. Moreover, the rump that remained was further stressed by financial institutions failing to provide reliable long-term loans on acceptable terms, so squeezing remnant producers and adding to the uncertainty of their survival. If this were not bad enough, finance had dealt another blow by encouraging consumer borrowing on a gigantic scale, especially for housing. This, he stated, was hugely distorting of economic activity generally, making the whole economy more fragile and underpinning the financial crisis of 2008 as well of that two months earlier.

Phillip Stapleton concluded the interview by saying that he looked forward to a complete rethinking of government economic policy, either by the present government or by a new one. There was a desperate need for a concentration on genuinely productive activity that focused on real commodities, so improving peoples living standards in a sustainable way. Stapleton made no further mention of the violent assassinations, only hoping that something good would emerge from the "events of Friday". No doubt, many members of the AUKM approved wholeheartedly of what had been said, but more than a few ministers of Jonathan Easton's government were shocked rigid. Indeed, a substantial number began to recalibrate, assessing the effects of Stapleton's remarks and their options for retaining their ministerial portfolios if the present government fell, and a new one was formed. Thus, there was induced not simply a crisis of legitimacy at the lower and middling rungs of society; it infected the higher ones too.

It was also on the Sunday that the sixth memorable event, or rather class of events, was also on display. They were from the very beginning the most shocking to the traditionally respectable members of British society even though there was no violence or illegal behaviour on offer. Instead, the offence was purely verbal. At the many Sunday services held in the places of worship of the Church of England, several leading churchmen and significant numbers of ordinary clergy referred to the assassinations of Friday and called for people to "take a balanced view" of the events of the previous two days. This was from a Church that had only recently still been referred to as 'the Establishment at prayer'. True, this description had been fraying for some years as the churchmen had embraced one progressive cause after another and several bishops had indicated that belief in the Christian God could be divisive and non-inclusive. But with this call for a balanced view of brutal assassinations, the Rubicon had been crossed for many of the 'great and the good' of British society. Moreover, it was reinforced later by no less than the Archbishop of Cantershire, who claimed that while Christian love was the best policy, it was *first* best, and there were *second-best* policies which could also display merit. He did not elaborate on what these might be but given the events of the preceding Friday, it was not difficult to make a connection that was valid or not. Likewise, with the Dean of St. Stevenshire, who made the argument that the commandments were "statements of advice" and should be interpreted as the context and consequences required. In particular, the sixth commandment should not be understood in a "unsophisticated, literal manner" but rather with regard to "the expected effects of its adherence or non-adherence."

So it was that society started dividing, and it was no exaggeration to characterize this as involving a 'great awakening'. Somewhat later, even members of The Committee recalled that they were surprised by their own success in the matter of promoting public support for their actions. They, too, had underestimated the depth of hostility to the prevailing order and also its breadth across most social classes. Naturally, there had been an expectation of some shows of support, but the scale and its diversity were especially heart-warming for them.

# III RESPONSE

At 10.00 a.m. on the Saturday morning, Charles Ryder met with the five leading members of the team of Special Branch detectives that he had begun to assemble the previous evening and continued with during the night. All had been working on other cases or were about to go on holiday, but there was no problem in getting them transferred or made available since his investigation into the assassinations had been prioritized by the Commissioner and was clearly of supreme importance. (And Charles Ryder held the same belief as Alexander Hendry that any hindrance would have proved a mistake for the Commissioner, not for the Commander). He explained that he would be in overall charge of the investigation and that the second tier would comprise the five Inspectors, each of whom would specialize in one of the assassinations but would not be limited to such. The other, lower ranked, officers could be assigned duties as required by all of them and, unless there was special need, they would not be attending the meetings between himself and the five leading detectives. Everyone would operate from the set of offices cordoned off in E wing of Scotland Yard, which were specially securitized and had direct communication lines to the security services and police authorities in the land. Budgetary constraints did not exist; what was needed would be supplied. And all governmental administration throughout the country were at their disposal for solving the crimes of the previous day.

Ryder introduced the leading team members even

though most knew each other already: Chief Inspector Beth Hamilton, Inspector Gordon Sinclair, Chief Inspector Harry Brown, Chief Inspector Eric Fowler, and Inspector John Simmons. He then summarized the events surrounding the murders that had brought them together and allocated initial responsibilities. Beth Hamilton was assigned the Sir Roger Gilchrest file, Gordon Sinclair was given the Stephanie Almiston case, Harry Brown received the Billy Jones assassination, Eric Fowler that of the James Stewart murder, and John Simmons got the Rory Candiman case. The Commander then set provisional times of meetings each day to report on progress and discuss the way forward. He also made it clear that those assembled would have but the most limited of private lives until success had been achieved and reminded one and all that they were to be free with their views irrespective of rank. He also added that he knew them all to be the very best officers of Special Branch, and that  he had every confidence in each and all and that he would back them to the hilt in the exercise of their powers, which were considerable given the proclamation of the state of emergency. Each could be in direct contact with all members of the team and had complete access to the large information base that was accumulating, and which would be added to continuously every day as was deemed appropriate. All of the five detectives also had private rooms available to them nearby, complete with a bed and full bathrooms, which they could choose to use if they lacked the time to journey to their homes in the evening or needed to rest during the day.

He then turned to summarizing the state of the investigation so far, which he saw as very much work in progress in every assassination, and stressed the need for each and all to keep abreast of the information in the data base as it was updated. However, he added that there was also material present that was not especially important and should not be a matter on which to focus. This was true, for example, of the autopsy results, which did not add anything of significance to what was obvious in the manner of the killings. When he had finished, the Commander opened the meeting to questions. Harry Brown, who had primary responsibility for the Billy Jones killing, asked what was on everyone's mind, "Who do you think was behind all this sir?"

"Obviously, that is *the* question, but we have no major leads at present," responded Ryder.

"So, to begin with, we should concentrate on old fashioned police work of treating each killing as a murder investigation."

"Yes and no, Harry," came the reply of the Commander. "Of course, we want to nail the actual killers, but these appear to be no ordinary killings, and those who are ultimately responsible are unlikely to be the actual killers. Nor are they likely to be the usual suspects in a typical murder investigation: family, friends, everyday-enemies, jilted lovers, and so forth. There are a range of possibilities, including political radicals, jihadists, the IRA, foreign intelligence services of hostile powers, organized crime syndicates, and so on. We have not ascertained anything definite at present. This also raises another question that needs to be explored. Why were these five bankers picked? Are there any connections between them or important commonalities? Or were they picked because they were deemed to be especially guilty of what the Committee regarded as heinous crimes? Maybe it was just a matter of being emblematically guilty in the eyes of the Committee. We simply do not know at this stage and need to find out."

With that, there were no more questions, and the meeting ended.

***

An hour later, Chief Inspector Beth Hamilton was reviewing the file on the assassination of Sir Roger Gilchrest in Office 2 of E wing. The file, which was building rapidly, described the killing and its location, provided initial Scene of Crime Officers (SOCO) findings, explained how access to the car was finally achieved, included the autopsy report and outlined the ongoing enquiries. There were also three items that had been filed in the previous hour. The first, a report from the local constabulary, stated that there appeared to be no witnesses either to the assassination or to the events surrounding it. The private CCTV footage at Sir Roger's home had clearly shown him entering the Bentley, apparently alone and driving out of the grounds, but there was no other CCTV coverage available since his route was not covered. The second, also from the area police, indicated that the south-western and north-eastern B2212 had been blocked off to motorists early the previous morning, so Sir Roger's car was likely the last to enter from his direction until the emergency services had been called later in the morning by another driver proceeding the opposite way. Having ignored the road blocking, the driver had thought it odd that a Bentley should be stationary with its engine running and with no response from the driver when he tapped on the window. So far, no other information had come to light as to any suspicious activity in the locale, but inquiries were continuing.

The third item was very much more interesting. Apparently, Sir Roger had provided details of the many innovative features of his car to both the local police and the Metropolitan police, including of the array of cameras contained in the car. These showed pictures from inside the Bentley at the time of the assassination, including some of Sir Roger's neck gushing blood immediately after the slicing of his trachea. But of much greater significance by far were the pictures of the man dressed as a policeman who had apparently carried out the assassination. There he was, a white man about forty years old, leaning into the car and speaking to the occupant shortly before cutting his throat. "Gocha!" exclaimed Beth and immediately ordered that the relevant pictures be circulated to all police forces and cooperating security services the world over, coupled to the request for information on the identity of the person, his location and criminal history.

Beth then phoned Lady Gilchrest, at this stage the only person she thought who might be able to shed some light on her husband's death, requesting that she travel to Scotland Yard as soon as possible. The Lady was none too pleased at the invitation, so Beth made it clear that she was only being polite in "requesting" her presence in London, that a police car would be at the house within half an hour, and that she would be arrested if there was any lack of co-operation. Naturally, this had the desired effect, and Lady Gilchrest became more obliging. Beth began to recognize the advantage of the Prime Minister initiating a state of emergency. She was by nature not especially authoritarian but most certainly disliked the titled, however high or low, believing that they could be exempted from their responsibilities according to their own convenience. And, if she were perfectly honest, she lacked respect for them more generally. Having been orphaned at the age of eleven, she was of an independent disposition. This too had been fostered by her uncle who had taken responsibility for her upbringing. He had discharged his duties very well indeed, even while becoming a successful businessman himself, and particularly so with regard to her education and in promoting confidence in herself. She was enormously grateful to him for all his love and support, but she had also used it well by working energetically. In her view, the titled too received much support but tended not to recognize it, while genuine work of any kind did not seem to be especially prominent in their lives either.

After leaving university, Beth had joined the police on a fast-track promotion program, then risen rapidly through the ranks by using her intelligence and energy, so foregoing many of the pleasures of ordinary life. Already a Chief Inspector at the age of thirty-two, she also knew that there was much farther to rise and gave off no impression to others of wanting to stop halfway. That had included cancelling her holiday when the Commander had telephoned yesterday evening to request her presence in the investigation and the postponement of her leave that was due to begin the following day. It also meant always presenting herself in the most attractive of ways, by dressing smartly and ensuring that her physical loveliness was not suppressed. There was clearly a resemblance to the young Audrey Hepburn, although Beth was taller and less slight. And with short black hair stylishly cut, an excellent figure and superb dress sense, no one could fail to notice her, and no man or woman would be ashamed to be seen with her anywhere. This was reinforced by the fact that she could be excellent company, being well-read, typically friendly and with a good sense of humour.

However, Beth was also different from most other people in a less obvious way. There was a deeper side to her. Not to put a too fine a point on the matter, she thoroughly disliked what she called the "air-head" quality of contemporary life in which consumerism orientated to endless shopping, mindless entertainments, junk food, alcohol and beach-holidays figured most prominently. Tattoos and piercings were not in short supply either. Typically, it all came along with promiscuous sexual relations and ignorance of anything culturally elevated, including of the nature of the society and the history that had produced it. Such unawareness meant most individuals possessed little capability to exercise genuine agency in the shaping of their own lives and instead followed tracks laid down for them by the narrow contexts in which they lived.

Beth made no secret of her views, and if ever asked to elucidate them would start with a quote from Shakespeare, "To Be, or not to Be," interpreting "To Be" to mean taking control of one's life, and "not to Be" as being overwhelmingly determined by external forces. However, she also pointed out that this was not a simple dichotomy because of the very nature of the human species. People were and would always be both determined and determining creatures, but it was the second quality that distinguished them from other animals. Putting aside biology, they were also molded by their environment, including the social environment. But at the same time, people had the capacity to attain an understanding and control of social relationships. Hence, the ideal of self determination would mean reforming society in a manner that brought the self closer to what it desired to be by remolding its social determinants.

She recognized this to be a complex notion made up of many dimensions and facing significant constraints. Obviously, it necessitated an understanding of the properties of the social relationships into which people are born, or as she sometimes expressed it "the bequest of history". Furthermore, self determination required knowledge of how these relations could be modified to form the self closer to what it wished to be, so the difference between the reality of what is and the ideal of what could be contracted. Moreover, this condition of agency needed the pressures of physical existence not be overwhelming, so conditions of affluence and the absence of war were essential. Poverty and armed conflict meant that virtually everything would be subordinated to the imperatives of survival, and agency was thereby swamped. However, in the case of modern Britain and many other countries, affluence and international peace prevailed, so democracy and a secure legal order allowed space for a self determination by the people. Democracy meant they could determine the properties of their collective, or public, or social life together. And a secure legal order defined by these properties provided an environment for choices over matters that were individual or private.

In contemplating all these conditions for the attainment of self determination, or freedom as it might be called, Beth's view was that the chief problems lay in ignorance of the first two conditions. Most people appeared not to understand the bequest of history and were even less knowledgeable of how the bequest could be molded into something more congenial for their own selves. She refused to believe that an "air head" life could be the choice of any rational being aware of its own determinants and possibilities. So, the prime objective was to repair the intellectual deficiency. However, she acknowledged that there was little a single individual could contribute here beyond helping to promote democracy and the legal order it generated, which were the pathways too agency for those who sought it. Thus, she had joined the police ten years earlier not just for reasons of career but because she considered the protection of democracy and the maintenance of orderly relations between individuals to be necessary conditions for creating a genuine human order. They together provided a basis for the determining component in human life to figure ever larger relative to the determined aspects, both at the collective and individual level. Democracy allowed a genuine collective choice over those shared conditions of life that affected one and all. The legal order so established by democratic means then provided the secure pathways for individuals to consciously mold themselves. However, it remained the case that the bulk of people appeared not to take advantage of this and confined themselves within air-head activities and consciousness, without any appreciation of what a more fulfilling life would look like. Beth remained somewhat puzzled as to why this was so and tended to get depressed when she thought about it for very long.

Furthermore, even colleagues with which Beth associated did not understand her perspective and sometimes simply dismissed it as a combination of elitism, snobbery and prudery. The only kindred spirit she had encountered in London was her friend Charlotte, and they met infrequently owing to the pressures work. Thus, while Beth could blend in well with her fellow police officers, it was also limited as she held to a philosophy they did not comprehend. Moreover, she, herself, was having doubts about it given the persistence of 'air head' behaviours and the lack of any degree of sophistication in much popular culture. Her perspective had also affected her emotional life. While she had had several serious love affairs over the years, none of the attractions had ever matured into a permanent relationship because the initial promise of an intellectual concordance had always petered out. Consequently, there was a profound sense of loneliness in her life. While the lack of attachment had allowed her time to keep well abreast of social and political matters, this was only an intellectual compensation for the lack of a continuing intimate relationship. Moreover, it had reinforced her belief that historical knowledge and awareness of the need for the understanding of genuine agency were essential components in any partner she would choose in the future, assuming of course that potential mates did appear, and she was far from certain any would.

***

Lady Gilchrest arrived about an hour and a quarter later. She was a distinguished looking woman but lacked physical attractiveness and carried herself as if others must always defer to her presence and needs. She was ushered into one of the interview rooms, and Beth met her with Charles Ryder five minutes later. She introduced herself and the Commander and, after expressing their condolences, proceeded with the interview. Beth began with the obvious question, "Have you any idea who may have been responsible for the death of your husband?"

"None whatsoever," replied the Lady.

"Did he have any enemies?"

"Thousands, I should think, perhaps millions; he was a truly awful person in every respect," was the immediate response, and Beth could not help noticing a faint smile on the face of Lady Gilchrest.

"Is there anyone who might have a better idea?" Beth responded.

"Well, you could try his mistress, Rosalind Gilchrest, his brother's wife and a well-known tart; I can let you have her address and telephone number. My late husband was probably going to have a session with her yesterday. He usually did on Fridays. Before her he had a variety of other women 'on the side' as they say. I can let you have at least some of their names, but I do not have the information to hand now."

The details were duly noted, after which Beth showed Lady Gilchrest the photograph of the assassin taken seconds before he struck, asking her whether she recognized the man.

"I cannot be sure, but he may have been one of the workers we have had at the house during the last month to relay the surface of the road. He looks somehow familiar and was obviously a very public spirited individual. If you do encounter him, please convey my thanks for his good work."

"You appear not to be taking any of this very seriously Lady Gilchrest," interjected the Commander, "Why is that?"

"Well, living with the bastard for over twenty years might have something to do with it. But I know truly little of his life outside the house and have no interest in finding out who killed him. I am not hiding anything, and I am, in fact, being as candid as I possibly can be. He had no redeeming features as far as I was concerned, and I detested him. I do not believe that there is any law against that, is there?"

Beth then provided a list of the other four bankers that had been killed the day before and asked whether Sir Roger had known them in any way at all.

"Not that I know of," she replied, "but if they were leading bankers, he may well have done so. I simply do not know. And if they were anything like my husband, they got what they deserved. I believe it is sometimes said of America that 'it has an exaggerated sense of innocence', but it is certainly true of senior bankers. They are wholly self-serving, yet believe they are the foundation of all wealth and property and are themselves not well done by."

Beth experienced a new degree of warmth for the lady but showed no change in her disposition.

"That was not very helpful," said Ryder immediately after he was alone with Beth. "Please get someone to check on the movements of Lady Gilchrest recently and to interview Rosalind Gilchrest, as well as obtain the list of other mistresses he may have had and interview them too. But these matters are just routine and are unlikely to shed any light on events, so I do not think either of us need to be involved directly at this stage. Our real break is the photograph of the killer, but I also doubt if we will be lucky enough for him to turn out to be just a local building labourer. However, we should make no unwarranted assumptions, and it is beginning to look as if the assassination were not quite as flawless as they appeared to be yesterday."

"I agree sir and will do."

***

If the murderer or murderers had made a mistake in the killing of Rory Candiman, the Vice President of Client Services at Floydsons, Inspector John Simmons could not see where it was. And he had had a lot of experience in investigating murders over three decades in the force. For the past two hours, he had been studying the file and all the updates. The people at the meeting in the apartment during the evening preceding the murder had been pretty well established, having been identified with the help of the staff at Floydsons Bank, as well as the computer and cell phone of the deceased. All would be brought in for interview, but since the death had occurred in the early morning, it is unlikely that much would be learnt. Nonetheless, fingerprints and DNA samples could be taken and matched with those found in the apartment. If this were done comprehensively, those of the assassins might be inferred from all the data collected. However, beyond this there was little of use. CCTV cameras in the lobby had shown a large number of people entering and exiting the hotel. They would be traced and interviewed as far as was possible, but at present the only persons who stood out were two comprehensively veiled Muslim women exiting at 9.55 a.m. on the Friday morning. While some of his colleagues on the investigation thought this significant, John Simmons, himself, put more weight on the fact that the CCTV cameras at one of the rear exits had ceased to function. The assassin, or assassins, could have come and gone without leaving any electronic record of entry and exit. But every possibility would be followed up, and officers had already begun interviewing those known to be in the building at about the time of death. At the very moment when he decided to get yet another cup of coffee, he received the call that Samantha Haineson, thought to be one of those at the meeting of the previous evening, had been brought into the Yard and was awaiting his attention in an interview room.

Simmons first observed her through the one-way glass. She was, to say the least, strikingly attractive, with an egg-timer figure and beautiful face accompanied by a superb cut of thick blonde hair, appearing to be in her early twenties, looking affluent and smartly dressed. As he entered the interview room, she smiled and shook his hand. He asked her to sit and explained why she had been brought in, sought to address any fears she might have, and told her she would be able to leave soon as long as she answered all of his questions with complete honesty. He began by asking who was at the meeting on Thursday evening, and what had transpired. A seasoned detective with liberal views, he was nevertheless somewhat shocked by how direct and candid was her reply.

"There were three other women present and three other men besides Rory Candiman. I can tell you only the names I knew them as, which were their first names. We had drinks and a meal, and the rest of the evening until about eleven was just sex. I assume the other three girls were, like me, paid handsomely and just had to accommodate whatever the men wanted. It had started off with each man pairing with a particular girl in one of the many bedrooms, but it very soon became an orgy. All the men had probably taken something to ensure they did not tire of events. They were certainly highly active. Shortly after 11.00 p.m. Rory called a 'halt to proceedings', which had in fact pretty much ended anyway, and the three other girls and the three men apart from Rory left, as I did. I went home, and I assume all other women did too or to hotels to meet more clients."

At this point, John Simmons noticed a message on the screen of his mobile phone informing him that Jimmy Crawford had just been brought in and was three doors down. So, he asked the obvious question, "We understand that a man named Jimmy was one of the other guests; is there anything that struck you about him?"

"Apart from him being the least attractive man in the place, bad breath and a truly catholic taste for all manner of couplings, I do not think so. He *did* rather than said but behaved pretty much the same as the other two male guests. The only civilized male there was Rory. He was always decent and could be a sensitive lover. I liked him, and I am sorry he is dead."

Simmons recognized that there was not much point pursuing the interview any further at this stage and simply asked, "Do you have any more information that you might imagine could be relevant to the investigation in any way?"

"I do not think so, and I have thought about it ever since I heard the news. However, I would like to add that while I appreciate that you disapprove of my activities, and for understandable reasons, I do need a great deal of money to support my university studies and my mother in a long term care home as a result of a stroke at an early age. I also know that this sounds very corny, but it is true, and both my studies and my mother are important to me, so, I make no apologies for my behaviour."

"Believe it or not Ms. Haineson, I do understand, and I appreciate your cooperation. I doubt if we will want to interview you again, but please keep us apprised of your location just in case. The female police officer who will come and collect you from this room will tell you what procedures to follow and write down the particulars of the other guests that you can remember, as well as take your fingerprints and a sample of DNA for purposes of elimination." With that John Simmons stood up, shook her hand, left the room, and went to the kitchen for his coffee.

Ten minutes later, when he observed Jimmy Crawford, he could not help feeling some sympathy for Samantha Haineson and the other women at the party. The man had no attractive features whatsoever and was also clearly agitated, explaining to the officer in the room that it was imperative that he catch his 3.05 p.m. train to Edinburgh as Mrs. Crawford would be very worried if he were to miss it. When he did enter the room, John Simmons approach was considerably less gentle than it had been with Samantha Haineson, "We have you on film from Thursday evening copulating with all and sundry and in multiple orifices. This will be made available to Mrs. Crawford in short order as well as your employer and colleagues, and charges will be laid unless you tell me everything you know about the events of that evening and how they might pertain to the murder of Rory Candiman."

This approach was clearly a mistake as Crawford became a blubbering wreak, and it took at least forty minutes for him to gain any composure. When he did, he could add little to what John Simmons already knew or had inferred, and he ended the interview very quickly. While there may be much of interest to the Fraud Squad and the Inland Revenue in the happenings of Thursday night, Simmons deduced that they had no relevance to the killing and the wider purposes which motivated it.

Much the same proved true when the other men and women present at the apartment on the Thursday evening were interviewed. All of the women were young and attractive and far from being common tarts, while the men were non-descript financial managers. And none could shed light on anything of relevance. Again, their activities were a matter for the Fraud Squad and the Inland Revenue, not Special Branch.

***

A slightly more optimistic assessment was being reached by Eric Fowler, who was handling the inquiry into the James Stewart killing on the Lanchester golf course. He was extremely thorough and intelligent in all that he did, both of which were attested by the fact that he was a Chief Inspector at the age of thirty six, even though he had not entered the force on a fast-track stream like Beth. Furthermore, his progress was even more impressive because he was neither especially personable nor attractive, again distinguishing himself from Beth. However, he was not envious of her and nor was he hostile to her. Quite the contrary, Eric Fowler was besotted by her. While always careful to maintain self-control and conform to conventional standards, he continually watched for any sign that she would welcome a more amorous approach on his part. None had so far been forthcoming. While she was always friendly towards him that was her disposition toward all colleagues and signified nothing about him being in any way special to her. Thus, Eric was becoming rather soured with life and especially depressed at his prospects on the emotional front. However, he tried not to let this interfere with his concentration and skills of detection.

As for the assassination on the golf course, although there was nothing useful so far, the investigation did have several possibilities. The regular golf caddie had been interviewed by local police, but all he could remember was opening his door on the Thursday evening to be greeted by two young women who had said they were conducting a survey, about what he could no longer remember. Of course, he had invited them inside, after which everything had gone blank because they quickly anesthetized him. He had but the vaguest recollection of what they looked like, although he did remember that he thought them attractive. A text message to James was found on his cell phone, explaining that he was unable to attend him on the Friday morning, so he had arranged for a substitute caddie.

The local police had no reason not to believe him, although they did find it suspicious when they searched the house that he had also 'forgotten' to mention the ten thousand pounds left by the women along with a note apologizing for any inconvenience they may have caused him and hoping that the money would compensate. Not surprisingly, the CCTV cameras at the Golf club had been disabled sometime during the night, but there was still the possibility that the club staff might be able to construct a likeness of the actual caddie with the police artist, and he was the most likely killer. It was also possible that the Scene of Crime Officers, (SOCO), could find shoeprints in the wood and tire tracks in the laybys, which might yield important information, along with interviews with motorists usually passing the area at the relevant time. But on all these matters, there was not much to do but wait, and he turned to reviewing the material on the other cases.

***

By contrast, Gordon Sinclair, the inspector reviewing the fatal shooting of Stephanie Almiston near the Barnes railway station drew only blanks and had little hope that anything of substance would emerge in due course. He, too, was an experienced detective noted for his tenacity and past successes in murder investigations. But in this case, there was little prospect of a breakthrough of any kind. It was obvious that Stephanie herself was a strikingly good-looking woman, and anything she did or was done to her would normally attract a great deal of attention. But there was truly little normal in the situation. The CCTV on the station and outside the station had been disabled during the night, and nobody so far contacted had seen anyone obviously doing so. Likewise, no witnesses to the murder had come forward. Some people remembered what they thought was a woman in a cape and hat entering the lane just before the time Stephanie must have been killed, but since she also had a scarf covering her lower face there would be no chance of constructing a likeness as the clothing worn completely disguised her. Michelangelo had been interviewed, but it was clear that he was broken-hearted and, more importantly for the investigation, was miles away at the time of the murder and had no resources to finance it. So, there really was nothing to go on, nor the expectation that anything would or could turn up. If the perpetrators of the five crimes were to be caught, it was most unlikely that it would be done through anything connected to the murder of Stephanie Almiston. The only possibility of this being wrong was that the assassin or assassins could have been seen in exiting the lane in which Stephanie was shot. Officers were interviewing residents in the area and posting notices to travelers to contact them if they had any information.

***

Harry Brown had very much better luck with the killing of Billy Jones. He was the longest serving officer of all the detectives and the senior Chief Inspector on the investigation. Heavy-set, overweight, and typically looking bad-tempered, he often came across as rude. But he was also astute in matters of police work and for people who got to know him a dependable friend. In the present case, several people who lived close to the location where Billy Jones was blown up reported having seen a helicopter circling the area for a few minutes before the explosion and then departing almost immediately after the fireball occurred. Hence, the local rental agency had been investigated, and all those bar two men who had hired machines covering the period of the assassination had been identified and eliminated from the investigation. The unidentified renters of a helicopter, therefore, became suspects, and here the police were fortunate. Although the CCTV cameras had been disabled at the helicopter hire premises, several other customers had inadvertently snapped the two suspects on their phones and tablets. The local constabulary in whose jurisdiction the airport lay had done a fine job in seeking out all those who were present at the relevant times, interviewing them and examining their cameras, phones and tablets. None of the pictures were very well defined, but the technicians were working to enhance their quality and were optimistic that they could eventually do so, although it would take some time to complete.

Harry had always taken the view that the propensity of people to create a record of all that they did was one of the more mindless qualities of digital age (when would they ever have time to look at it all?), but he was recognizing its benefits in this particular instance, especially as there was nothing else that seemed worth pursuing. The identification documents provided to the helicopter rental firm were probably stolen or forged, and the employee organizing the transaction remembered no distinguishing characteristics of the two renters, while forensics had found nothing obviously useful in the helicopter they had rented. But sometimes the police got very lucky, and this seemed to be one of those times when the neurosis of the general public to preserve all they did in pictures had actually created something of value.

***

At 1.05 p.m. Charles Ryder knocked and immediately entered Beth's office. "We have got an ID on the assassin of Gilchrest. He is being held by the Federal Security Service, or, as the organization is more usually known, the FSB, in Moscow. I do not know the details, but I have just spoken to a Colonel Andrei Chekhov, who has no doubt that he is the man we want. He will meet you off the plane that leaves for Moscow at 2.20 p.m. this afternoon. There is a car waiting to take you home for your things and then to Heathrow where you will enter the plane directly through the secured passage."

"That's great," exclaimed Beth, "but I need some guidance. What happens if he will not talk? What can I offer him in the way of inducements?"

"Legally, close to nothing at all, but do what you have too, and I will ensure that the agreement sticks," responded Ryder. "We need a break Beth, and this is the best we have at the moment. Keep in close touch, but you have my full authority to do whatever you believe is necessary."

"Ok sir, I will do as you say and keep you posted," replied Beth. She had tremendous respect for Charles Ryder, knowing that with fellow officers his word was his bond. She also had to admit that she found him most attractive in all other ways as well and often thought it a great pity that he was married and especially to her closest friend in London. Therefore, it was out of the question for there to be anything more than collegial relations with Charles. At most, decency and propriety allowed only an extension to personal friendship outside of work. As a consequence, she was always careful to remain professional, but the fact that Ryder put so much confidence in her made attraction to him even stronger.

Normally, the journey by car from the Yard to her apartment in Richmond took over an hour, but the police car with sirens at full strength did it in twenty-five minutes, albeit aided by police officers halting other traffic where required. It took Beth less than ten minutes to put together a travel bag good for a couple of days and then another thirty minutes to get to Heathrow. She was on the plane in the last row of first class at 2.17 p.m., three minutes before it was due to leave the gate.

***

The flight was uneventful; the passenger next to her was quiet, and the cabin crew helpful but not intrusive. Beth was thus able to collect her thoughts and formulate a provisional plan of action. She was not nervous but more intrigued by the thought of cooperating with the FSB, the successor to the KGB. She knew the organization's reputation as one of the four best security services in the world, perhaps the best, rivaled in effectiveness only by the CIA, MI6 and Mossad. And she also knew that relations between the UK and Russia had warmed somewhat since the low points reached after the differences over the Ukraine, the murders in Salisbury, and the allegations of electoral interference. The government of both countries appeared to want the warming to continue, and it seemed not a day passed without another announcement of cooperation in some new endeavour. So, hopefully, there would be no gaming by the Russians, and everything would be straightforward including extracting information from the assassin. But that was a hope; she expected far less and focused on what she might do about that.

However, as the flight was nearly four hours long, her thoughts extended beyond the investigation and embraced Russian matters more generally. She had taken several courses on the history and culture of the country at university and found it all fascinating. Her admiration of Russian literature and Russian arts more generally was not, of course, exceptional. It was a widely shared judgement in the West and extended into the Soviet period, even including some who were ferociously anti-communist. However, she had a distinct perspective on the history of modern Russia that had been greatly influenced by one of her more theoretically inclined professors. He had emphasized that this was a "concentrated history" in which happenings were both extreme and compressed in time, and usually having dramatic outcomes. And it was confirmed when the course continued with an account of the events. The *ancien regime* of Tsarism had no prospect of surviving once the First World War began with the attack by German forces. The Russian defenders faced the much more modern armies of the invaders, and their casualties rose to over seven million within three years. By 1917, the Russian military forces were also disintegrating as supply chains collapsed, and desertions rose rapidly. With the success of the Bolshevik revolution of that year, which was heavily supported by the troops, the country escaped conquest by Germany only by ceding vast areas of land in the west of the country. But the revolution also provoked a civil war, in which many western powers intervened against the Bolsheviks and their supporters. This conflict claimed another ten million lives before the revolutionaries ultimately prevailed.

By the early 1920s, the country was near complete ruin, and economic recovery was achieved only via policies that hugely incentivized and benefitted the peasantry, who continued to produce in the traditional premodern fashion. But this could not and did not last long. Both internal threats to the Bolshevik regime and external threats to the country made rapid economic growth and military modernization imperative. They each hinged on state control of agriculture in the form of the collectivization of the peasantry, which allowed extraction of the agricultural surplus and much increased investment in industry and the military through central planning, even though it was bitterly resisted by the peasants and involved many millions of casualties. However, there is no doubt that without collectivization and the increased investment it facilitated, the Nazi invasion of 1941 would have succeeded in conquering the whole country. As it was, Russian casualties in World War Two were around twenty-six million, and the economic destruction was huge. However, victory in 1945 also resulted in a Russian empire in eastern Europe that finally brought secure borders.

The coercion involved in the collectivization of the peasants, central planning and war ensured that internal conditions in Russia could only be describes as totalitarian from the 1930s on, as the state was the mobilizing force throughout. However, after Stalin's death in the early 1950s, internal conditions did become more civilized and prosperous for ordinary Russians. But, concurrently, the so-called liberalization also brought a mushrooming of corruption followed by much slower rates of growth, ultimately contributing to the disintegration of the eastern empire and the Soviet Union itself in the early 1990s. Nonetheless, both continued military modernization and corruption remained prominent features of post-Soviet Russia, and it was only with Yevgeni Kovalny becoming president two years ago that the latter began to be eliminated. Russia was now a cleaner and freer country, although its overall military situation had deteriorated somewhat compared to that prevailing in the Soviet Union owing to the expansion of NATO. This western military organization had always presented itself as being purely defensive and embodying all the decencies of life, but even Russians with only a passing acquaintance with the history of its principal members would recognize the self-description as little more than propaganda. Given their own past encounters, who could blame them. However, it was also true that holding to this perspective allowed them to take some comfort from the recent fraying of the western alliance and improving relations with Britain that had begun some years ago under the Trump presidency in the United States.

Most of these events had figured in Beth's courses on Russian history, but she had at one point asked her tutor for some elaboration on the significance of his term "concentrated history". While she understood well enough that it described events happening rapidly and intensely, she wanted to know if there was a deeper and more general causal process involved. Her professor had been impressed by the question itself because it suggested the need on her part for some more profound theoretical understanding, and he did her the service of answering in a concise and illuminating manner that she had never forgotten. The stress was placed on the process of modernization occurring in different countries at different times, and frequently the laggards were placed under severe stress militarily by the more advanced powers. This was certainly true for Russia at the beginning of the twentieth century because of its location adjacent to Europe, and the vast natural resources promised to any conqueror. The alternatives placed before Russian rulers were either collapse and colonization or attempt a modernizing response at rapid speed, and it was this threat and response that had produced the "concentrated history".

Beth had never forgotten this encounter even though it was brief. More importantly, she had taken it to heart, thinking thereafter not only historically in terms of events, but also theoretically in seeking generalizations arising from the interactions occurring as a result of the interests, vulnerabilities and interdependencies of the powers involved. It had also transformed her into an idealist who believed that history could teach lessons allowing a reorganization of human life for the better. Thus, not surprisingly, Beth thought Moscow might prove an interesting visit quite aside from dealing with the FSB and one of the assassins, although she recognized it was most unlikely that time would be in much supply. Nevertheless, it would be an experience that might be but the first of many in Russia. The opportunity to visit Moscow had certainly recharged her interest in the country.

# IV REPOSITIONING

Less than four hours after takeoff the flight began its descent into Sheremetyevo airport. Being two hours ahead of Britain, there was little to view except of the lights, but it appeared to be a fine night. The descent and landing were rapid, and the plane met its assigned gate at exactly 8.10 p.m. Beth immediately stood up, retrieved her bag and was led by the senior steward to the exit; the first passenger to leave and with the others held for a few minutes in the plane behind her. Immediately on walking through the bend in the passageway of the arm extending into the terminal, she saw him waiting for her, seemingly in his late thirties, appearing to be very fit, casually elegant in dress, and with a handsome face and a full head of dark hair. Beth saw a resemblance to Charles Ryder immediately. Indeed, he could have been a slightly older sibling of the very same. He smiled as he held out his hand to greet her, "Welcome to Moscow Chief Inspector, I am Andrei Chekhov, and I have a car waiting to take you to your hotel. We can chat on the way, and I can fill in some of the details."

"Call me Beth please Colonel, I appreciate you meeting me."

"Likewise, please call me Andrei; it is no trouble at all."

Andrei then took Beth toward one of the many nondescript doors, entered a code and traversed through several corridors that Beth thought bore a striking resemblance to those she had entered in Heathrow before she had boarded the plane. On exiting, they were met by the car that immediately proceeded into the central Moscow. During the journey, the Colonel explained the situation as it presently stood, "We arrested Nikolay Rayevsky earlier today. He was travelling on a Kazakh passport under a false name, but he was wanted by us, and it was facial recognition technology which alerted us to his arrival in Sheremetyevo despite his attempt at disguise. He was arrested shortly thereafter, and he is now at our Lubyanka headquarters in central Moscow. I do not propose we go there now, as we need to talk about what the FSB knows of him, and what you exactly want from him, as well as the best way to proceed from there."

"Yes indeed," said Beth, somewhat relieved that the encounter would be postponed until she was fresher.

"Good, we will go to your hotel, the Metropol, which is close to the Lubyanka. It is an old hotel that was finished in 1907 and has played an important role in Russian history. For example, Lenin frequently met with the Supreme Soviet there after the revolution, and Leon Trotsky lived in the hotel off and on between 1918 and 1920. But it is now totally modernized, and I think you will find it extremely comfortable. You are already booked in for two nights, but of course this can be extended or shortened as needed. And I have taken the liberty of reserving a small dining room, so we can have a light supper when we arrive and continue our discussion in a more pleasant environment."

"That is very kind of you Colonel – sorry, Andrei."

"It is the least we can do. But I am afraid that I will have to beg your indulgence until we arrive at the hotel, as there are some phone calls I have to make."

"Please feel free, I have to send an email to my boss, Commander Ryder, letting him know how things are," and with that she switched on her phone, while Andrei began to speak into his.

***

At around the time Beth was landing in Moscow, Charles Ryder was once again accessing the data base for any updates, when his phone rang. He was informed that he was speaking to one of the operators at Number 10, and the Prime Minister wished to talk to him. He was to remain on the line, and the PM would be with him very shortly.

About seven minutes later he heard the voice of Jonathan Easton, "I apologize for the delay Commander, thank you for waiting. I just wanted to get an update directly from you as to progress. I know it is early days, but you know the seriousness of the situation, and the social disorder engendered by the assassinations seems to worsen by the hour."

"Of course, sir. It is early in the investigation, but we certainly have some progress. The assassin of Sir Roger Gilchrest has been identified. He is being held by the Russian security services, and to be more precise by the FSB, and they informed us shortly after they received the pictures of the assassin from us. I sent my best officer to Moscow immediately, and she will probably be interrogating him in the morning, local time. The FSB appear to be very cooperative."

"Excellent, I will call President Kovalny early tomorrow morning and request that he ensure that those involved provide as much cooperation as is possible. I am sure he will try to help. Is there anything else?"

"We do have some leads on a couple of the other killings," responded Ryder, "but they are not as yet so fully formed."

"OK, that is good to know too", and with that the Prime minister wished the Commander, "Goodnight."

At that point Ryder received the email from Beth, explaining that she had arrived in Moscow, been met by Colonel Chekhov, and that she would be interviewing the assassin Nikolay Rayevsky in the morning after talking to Chekhov as to how best to proceed.

***

Twenty-five minutes after leaving the airport, the car pulled into the Metropol hotel's driveway. They were greeted by one of the managers, who gave Beth her room number and electronic key, undertook to have her bag sent to the room immediately, and informed her that a wake-up call for 7.00 a.m. had already been ordered. With that, they were taken to a small and elegant dining room, where an assortment of foods was already in place: cured salmon, pancakes, and caviar, borodinski bread, and a bottle of champagne on ice.

Beth began the conversation immediately after they were alone, "The more you can tell me about Rayevsky the better, but what I want from him is amazingly simple. I need him to tell me everything he knows about the assassination he undertook, what he knows about the other four assassinations and, especially, those who organized the assassinations."

"That is what I had assumed," responded Andrei, "and the FSB will extend full cooperation to you. Let me begin by giving you some background on him, and as it turns out on myself, since I have known him for over ten years."

"Yes, please do," said Beth, a little shocked.

"We were both recruited into the FSB from Russian Special Forces about ten years ago, so we were in the same cohort and did much training together, although we never became close friends. He specialized in field work and, not to put too fine a point on it, in covert operations involving assassinations. In contrast, I specialized in counterintelligence. He speaks English very well. In fact, my mother was a professor of English at Moscow State University and knew his father who was also a professor in the same department."

"Your English certainly is truly excellent," interjected Beth. "I had assumed his would be by the very nature of the killing he undertook in Britain."

"Yes, indeed, my mother was and still is a superb teacher, as was his father, and Rayevsky is good at languages and much else besides. He is intelligent and can be quite charming as well as violent. Being a top-notch assassin requires all such skills these days, and he always took pride in his work. But he deserted the FSB rather than leaving the service through the normal channels and went freelance several years ago; that is why we arrested him. And we were lucky. He was returning to Moscow to visit his father, who was dying, and he took a huge risk in doing so. But his father was – he died this evening, although we have kept this from Rayevsky – the only person he ever really loved."

"Will Rayevsky cooperate with my investigation?" asked Beth.

"That depends. We have to make it worthwhile to him. It is not just you or the British authorities being willing to make a deal with him because he will be more concerned to make an agreement with the FSB. After all, we hold him; there is yet still no extradition treaty with the UK, and we have obvious interests in what happens to him. So, the negotiation may be complex, I am afraid. But I hasten to add that the FSB will be as accommodating as it can be and will assist in bringing to account all those involved in the five assassinations. Our government is extremely interested in having better relations with the British, and for what it is worth, I am something of an anglophile."

Beth smiled and said, "I'm awfully glad to hear that. For my part, I have always been a fan of Russian culture. I took several courses in Russian history and literature at university and have never lost my love of either, and especially not of Pushkin, or of Chekhov for that matter," smiling as she said this.

"I, too, am incredibly pleased to hear that. For many years there has been much misunderstanding of all that is Russian in the West, and, of course, the converse applies too."

"What does the FSB want from Rayevsky, and how is it likely to run contrary to what I need. I understand that you have a legitimate interest in him, but I need to know what that is if we are to be able to come to a concordance."

"Indeed, but let us eat and then I will try to explain the main points."

***

Beth woke at 6.30 a.m. local time, after a good seven-hour sleep. She quickly showered, made up, dressed, and then went to the restaurant just off the hotel lobby for breakfast, where she also checked her phone for emails. There appeared to be none of real importance to her at present, and as she viewed her surroundings was again reminded of how beautiful the hotel was, almost wholly given over to Art Nouveau styles and brilliantly blended with ultramodern facilities. God knows how much it cost to stay here, she thought, but that was not her concern. Uppermost in her mind was what Andrei had told her of the interest that the FSB had in Rayevsky. Most particularly, they did not want him leaving Russia ever again without their authorization, and some punishment for his desertion had to be exacted. Normally, that would be severe, but there was room for negotiation with him regarding his cooperation on the British assassinations and on matters the FSB needed information, which was left unspecified. "He is not in a strong bargaining position," Andrei had said, "but it is somewhat stronger because of the British connection, and he will try to use this as leverage in his negotiations with us." He had then warned her that he might have to appear very unreasonable and quite vicious when they interrogated Rayevsky, but he also had hastened to assure her that he knew what he was doing, and that the Russian government and the FSB took British interests very seriously.

So, Beth concluded, the long and the short of the matter was that she had little to offer Rayevsky and was almost completely in the hands of the Russians. She believed Andrei when he said that they wished to be cooperative with the British, but how this would play out was far from clear. The FSB had an agenda about which she knew little while Colonel Chekhov could obviously be as tough as he was charming. And, as that thought left her, she saw him in the lobby with an attractive young blonde woman who had embraced him and was now waving her goodbyes as she exited the hotel. After his final wave, the Colonel looked round the hotel lobby and moved toward the dining room when he recognized her. Beth rose and smiled, asking him to join her for a cup of coffee since the time was only 7.40 a.m., and they had agreed the previous evening to meet at 8.00 a.m. that morning.

After taking a seat, Andrei enquired as to her night's sleep and comfort, hoping that she was well rested and fresh. "Indeed," she responded, "couldn't be better. It is a beautiful and comfortable hotel." They chatted a little about its significance in Russian history and culture before he suggested that they walk to the Lubyanka as it was not far, and it was a splendid morning, so at least she would be able to see some of the sites of Moscow.

"That is an excellent idea," answered Beth, "I would

like that very much." She finished her coffee, checked that his cup was empty, and suggested that they should go immediately.

"Good, you can see the Bolshoi Theatre close up just a couple of hundred meters further along the street."

As they walked, Andre explained, "I used to go to the Bolshoi frequently, but my attendance has tapered off in the last few years."

"You are a devotee of the ballet and opera? Are you too busy now?"

"Yes, I love the arts", but I can no longer go as easily as in the past when my wife worked there."

"She has changed her occupation?"

"No, she died of cancer five years ago. We were awfully close, and I get terribly maudlin when I now enter the Bolshoi. But I sometimes still go with my daughter, Sasha. Perhaps you saw her with me in the lobby of the hotel, which she likes very much. That is why she came in with me on her way to meet her university friends in a cafe. She always says the hotel makes her feel better about life."

"I am sorry to hear of your wife's death. I should not be so inquisitive. Being a detective breeds bad habits sometimes."

"No, not at all, I also know you have not come to Moscow for enjoyment, but, if I can, I would like the trip to be as pleasant as possible, and the Bolshoi is such a beautiful building; it would be a shame to miss it."

When she saw the theatre, Beth could only agree. It was truly magnificent. But she became aware also that she was relieved that the young blonde woman she had glimpsed earlier in the hotel was not Andrei's lover. That awareness made her a little nervous.

***

It was 6.15 a.m. in London when Beth was admiring the Bolshoi. Some detectives were still present in E wing, processing information. It was then that the enhanced photographs of the assassins of Billy Jones were uploaded to the data base. And they appeared to be particularly good, both in resolution and the variety of angles displayed. An email was immediately sent to Beth with all the photographs attached.

***

As she and Andrei arrived at the Lubyanka, he explained the importance of the building for the KGB and the FSB. It had been the headquarters of Felix Dzerzhinsky's security organization, the CHEKA, set up immediately after the Bolsheviks had come to power in 1917 and self-described as the 'Shield of the Revolution', plaques of which were still visible on all exterior walls. Beth listened politely, and she was genuinely interested, but she could not help wondering as to the significance of Andrei's' words in the light of the very obvious fact that there had been a counter-revolution in the early 1990s. However, she quickly suppressed the attraction to explore the logic of the matter, and they proceeded inside, where she gained an entrance pass, and took an elevator down into one of the basement floors of the building. As they did so, Andrei explained that Rayevsky would be in an interview room with two guards and a secretary, who would record all that was said in Russian and in English. A copy of this would be provided to her very shortly after the interrogation had been completed, so there was no need for her to take notes beyond what she thought especially significant. Nor should there be any difficulties in doing so as virtually everything would be in English. Also, Rayevsky could be no danger to her as he was restrained by ankle braces attached to the floor and a belt secured to the chair, which was itself immobile. And most likely, he would behave in a relatively friendly manner, so everything should be fairly normal or as normal as circumstances allowed. Andrei also pointed to a viewing window whereby she could observe Rayevsky, but he could not see her, and he advised Beth to use it before going into the room, so that she would know what to expect before beginning asking him questions. She did so. He was clearly the man in the photographs taken from the Bentley, although the pictures were rather kind to him compared to how he now appeared. He looked older than his years, somewhat ruffled and generated the impression of having gone to seed.

Rayevsky smiled when she and Andrei entered the room, introduced himself in English and apologized for not standing to greet her with a handshake. Andrei simply nodded at him and indicated to Beth that she should begin with her questions. She did so and in a very straightforward manner, "Mr. Rayevsky, we know you killed Sir Roger Gilchrest because we have photographs of you doing so, as you can see on my computer screen. What I wish to know is who else was involved, who took out the contract, and for what purpose. There were also assassinations of four other bankers shortly after that of Sir Roger Gilchrest, and I also wish to know all of what you can tell me about these too."

Rayevsky smiled once again, "Well, at this time, all information I have is for me to know, and you to guess. What I will tell you depends on what is offered to me in return for my cooperation. However, as a gesture of goodwill, one of my thoughts is not conditional at all Chief Inspector. I knew the detectives of Scotland Yard were clever, but I never realized how deliciously attractive they could be too. You really are so very ravishing."

Andrei told Rayevsky to behave himself, and Beth simply ignored the remark. Instead of responding, she showed a willingness to negotiate, "If you are completely honest with me, I can promise that the British will not seek extradition, so you will face no charges in a British court."

"But this is not enough, although that is no fault of yours Chief Inspector. I am at the mercy of the FSB, and only they can give me what I want. What do *you* propose Andrei?"

"As you know only too well, we could make life very unpleasant for you if you do not cooperate, and we also have our own interest in you being punished for desertion and not regaining your freedom for some considerable time. However, we are willing to be flexible if you do co-operate. I have been authorized to make you the following offer for your full cooperation on British matters and on those distinct matters that the FSB has an interest in." Andrei paused for a moment to let his words sink in, and then continued, "You will never leave Russia again without FSB permission; you will spend five years in prison, and you will lose the money in your foreign bank accounts."

Rayevsky laughed once again, "Not enough Andrei; you must know that. I propose instead that I will remain in Russia unless the FSB agrees to my leaving, and that I lose my normal freedoms for two years but only under house arrest, and that I keep half of the money in my bank accounts."

Andrei did not look pleased, "I do not think this or anything close to this will be possible, but I must check with General Dorov, so please excuse us. With that Beth was ushered out of the interview room and deposited in a cafe on the same floor, while Andrei went about his business. The surroundings were surprisingly pleasant judged by the facilities at Scotland Yard, and one of the waitresses spoke good English and was attentive to her needs. It was also quiet, so Beth checked her phone for any communications, transferred information to her computer and wrote down some notes of the proceedings so far, as well as trying to figure out what she could do if the FSB would not meet Rayevsky's terms.

As it turned out her wait was over two hours, but Andrei was in a far better humour when he returned to the cafe. "Good news. It is all agreed. President Kovalny himself has placed his stamp of approval on everything required to get Rayevsky to talk. We can now begin the interview proper. But let us first have an early lunch, and we will meet with Rayevsky again at 12 noon."

"Well there is a god after all," thought Beth as she turned to understand the lunch menu, which also seemed somewhat superior to what was usually on offer at the Yard.

***

Meanwhile, there were developments in the other investigations. John Simmons had interviewed the three other women at the 'party' of Rory Candiman, and one of them said Rory had mentioned to her that there was no possibility of anyone staying all night as the cleaners were due to arrive at 9.45 the following morning. Since there was no evidence of the apartment actually having been cleaned, Simmons took this to be very significant and deduced that it was most likely a pair of women that the investigation needed to concentrate attention on. This would be done when all CCTV data was reviewed again, and all members of the company with the cleaning contract needed to be interviewed. That was not much to go on, but it was better than nothing.

Some progress was also made in the investigation of the killing of James Stewart. SOCO had found several sets of fresh footprints in the woods leading to the road, and analysts were in the process of deducing what they could from the information in the molds. They worked on the assumption that every trace left evidence, and they were very frequently correct in thinking so. Additionally, extensive inquiries conducted by the local police had found several drivers who remembered seeing a car parked in the closest layby to the golf course around the time the assassin would have finished his task and made his getaway. Most of these drivers thought the car was a black Ford Focus, and one driver believed the numbers in the registration were 451, the same as his own. Consequently, extensive enquiries had been launched to find the car, and SOCO were also assiduously examining all the tire tracks in the layby itself.

The murder of Stephanie Almiston also possibly had a new lead, as two members of the public remembered seeing a woman in a long cape getting into a car outside the station, which they both thought peculiar as the morning was warm, and she was clearly overdressed. However, neither could shed much light on the car, other than one saying it looked like a taxi, so all local taxi companies and their drivers would now be interviewed for relevant information.

***

At 12 noon precisely, Andrei and Beth entered the interview room again. Andrei began by congratulating Rayevsky on the fact that his proposal had been accepted. He would never leave Russia without FSB approval, would be placed under house arrest for two years and retain only half the money in his foreign bank accounts if he *fully* cooperated on the British matters and on those other matters of concern to the FSB. He passed over a sheet of paper stating all this signed by the relevant authorities. Rayevsky read this very closely and, satisfied that all was in order, turned to Beth with a smile and said, "Fire away Chief Inspector; I will help as much as I can."

She began, "Do you admit killing Sir Roger Gilchrest?"

"Yes."

"Who else was involved in the assassination?"

"Those who undertook the contract were myself and two members of my team: Ivan Morozovic and Oxana Solomatic. Both are known to the FSB, and I am sure they will give you all the information they have, but I suspect they are no longer in Britain. Both had South African passports, which I think is where they live when not working. I could also give you the phone numbers and email addresses I used to contact them, but I suspect these will no longer be operational if they know I have been arrested. However, you may get lucky."

After Rayevsky had written down this information, Beth continued, "Were there no others involved?"

"Yes, but they knew nothing of what was to take place; they thought it was just a prank. I had worked at the Gilchrest manor as a building labourer for a couple of weeks to familiarize myself with Sir Roger – we wouldn't want to have had the wrong man assassinated, would we?" replied Rayevsky, and smiled. "Whilst there I arranged with the work crew leader, whose name was Brian Lane, to provide his crews' services for blocking and unblocking the road. I know only the first names of the five in the crew, and I will write them down for you."

"Who took out the contract?"

"Well, as our American friends say that is the $64,000 question, and I have very limited knowledge." Rayevsky then explained at length all the details of how he was contacted, communicated with and paid. Everything seemed to have been designed to hide the identity of those organizing the assassination, and he had never actually met the man he communicated with. All Rayevsky could offer was that he thought him "intelligent and well educated." He was also a man who was informed on Sir Roger's movements and "impeccably honest" in that payments were made exactly as had been initially agreed, and one in advance of the actual killing. As for the purpose of the assassination, Rayevsky had not enquired, and, at the time, he was unaware that four other assassinations would also take place. But he also hypothesized that those organizing the killings were "peculiar" in that they had placed a firm condition on everything; no one other than Sir Roger was to be harmed even if this meant aborting the operation. Rayevsky then continued with an outline of the other details of his contract and its fulfillment.

When he had finished, Andrei suggested they break for coffee, and he and Beth left the interview room for the café once again. As they took their seats, he asked, "Well, what do you think so far?"

"Pretty good. He is giving lots of information, and if it is true, it should help our investigation. I haven't spotted any lies, and some of the things he has said correspond to information I have from Gilchrest's wife, which he probably could not anticipate, so the omens are good that he is being honest."

"I agree, and I am sure he is being honest. If he were later shown to have lied, the deal we offered him would be null and void, and he knows this. I called for a coffee break to compare notes and to reassure you that I think he is keeping to his end of the bargain, which is not surprising as he *has got a real bargain*."

Twenty minutes later, they were back in the interview room, and the questions began again. Beth probed for more details on the assassination of Sir Roger, but nothing of substance beyond what had already been said emerged. She then turned to the other assassinations. She explained in considerable detail the facts of the assassinations of Rory Candiman, James Stewart, Stephanie Almiston and

Billy Jones. Rayevsky listened intently, as did Andrei, making some notes and interjecting at various points requesting elaboration. When she had finished, he admitted that he had no firm information, only "more or less informed hypotheses." He suspected that there were at least two women involved in the Stewart case, probably either Spanish or Italian and posing as cleaners, since garroting was a favoured model of killing in these two countries. They likely entered and exited through the back door where the CCTV cameras had been disabled. He provided a list of five names that he thought might be "persons of interest", a phrase he used with a broad smile on his face. But he was unwilling to wholly discount the importance of the two Muslim women who had left the building through the front entrance, although he doubted that jihadists were involved. If they were indeed the assassins, or otherwise implicated in the assassination, dressing as Muslims was most likely done to confuse any subsequent investigation.

As for the James Stewart case, his thoughts were a bit more definite because, he reasoned, there were not too many skilled swordsmen in the world and among them even fewer assassins who worked on contract. Moreover, he emphasized that to decapitate someone quickly required a great deal of skill no matter how easy it appeared to be. He thought only two people could do this, one a Turk by the name of Akif Bayram, and the other was French who was usually known as Bin Binot, but he stressed that these were only the names he knew them by, and he had no idea where they were. By contrast, Rayevsky believed that virtually anyone "in the trade" could have carried out the assassination of Stephanie Almiston because it was "so simple and straightforward." Then he added something which Beth took to be of significance, although the full import would only become clear to her much later. "I do not think the modalities of the killings are of secondary importance. In my own case, I was under strict instructions to kill in a particular way, at a particular time and particular location, while making absolutely sure no one else was harmed. Maybe it was different for the others, but if so, what was so special about Gilchrest? My advice is to work on the assumption that nothing in any of the assassinations was left to the discretion of those who carried them out. But why this was so is unclear."

When Rayevsky turned to consider the Jones case, he became more definite once again. He thought it the most complex of all the killings as the explosives would have had to have been placed in the car. After Beth interjected with the information that it had been in a garage for a service the previous day and remained there overnight, he responded with "there you have it, but how did the organizers know that this would be the case and how could they arrange to have the explosives added?" He then continued, arguing that this was, as with the Stewart case, accomplished by a couple of specialized operators, most likely Vladimir Romanovitch, a Russian with passable English, and Ernst Schneideral, a German with excellent English. But he added: they could be assuming any one of a large number of identities. At which point, Beth flipped open her computer, revealed the photographs of the two men who had hired the helicopter, and asked him if he knew them. Rayevsky laughed and responded, "The taller one is Romanovitch, and the shorter is Schneideral; it seems I must congratulate myself on my own detection abilities. Maybe my talent was helped by reading so much Sherlock Holmes as a child. I always enjoyed Conan Doyle's stories, how about you Chief Inspector?"

Beth did not respond to the question and said instead, "It is all beginning to sound as if it is a Russian operation".

Andrei looked askance, but Rayevsky smiled again

and countered her suggestion, "Perhaps, but I very much doubt it. The fact that Russians are involved in the assassinations is not especially significant and certainly does not imply that the Russian government is involved. My team and I, along with the others we now know were participants, are market players. The West did a great deal to introduce the market in Russia, and your propagandists have long proclaimed its efficiency properties to the point of convincing many Russians. The assassinations just delivered services demanded by those with the requisite purchasing power. In other words, we were just conforming to consumer preferences." Rayevsky smiled again.

Shortly after this the interrogation ended, with Andrei reminding Rayevsky that the agreement he had made with the FSB was for *complete information*, so if anything further occurred to him, he had to reveal it. He also made clear that he would be expected to be fully cooperative if any further questions arose. For her part, Beth thanked Rayevsky for his cooperation, knowing full well that she was only being polite and under no illusion that she had been dealing with anything other than an extremely dangerous psychopath.

***

Later, while they were drinking tea in the cafe a small package was delivered to Andrei, who passed it over to Beth saying, "This is an electronic record of the interview with Rayevsky". She immediately sent the data to Ryder, together with a short explanation of where the most significant information would be found, and an account of the information Rayevsky had written down for her. By then, the local time was 4.20 p.m., and Andrei suggested that they walk back to the Metropol together and meet later for dinner. He knew a French Bistro close to Red Square which he thought she would like, and its location would also allow her to see some more of the sites of Moscow. She could then get a good night's rest before catching her flight at midday on Monday. Transport to the airport had already been ordered, and he would also accompany her all of the way to the plane, so there was no need for her to make any arrangements.

"You are taking excellent care of me Andrei. I appreciate it so much, and I am very thankful for all your help with Rayevsky. We got more than I anticipated, and the information could be a key to cracking the case. Of course, I would love to have dinner with you. Nothing would please me more," and she smiled.

***

The restaurant, *Sweet Charm of the Bourgeoise,* turned out to be excellent in all respects and the dinner was superb. But, above all, it was Andrei's company that Beth found most attractive. There was no more discussion of the assassinations, and the conversation roamed widely. Andrei was obviously well educated and widely read, appeared to have had a most interesting life, and exhibited a developed sense of humour that dovetailed with her own. But she knew that she was good company too, and Andrei seemed to be enjoying the evening as much as herself. However, not everything was simply light and entertaining, and this suited them both as they each considered discussing more substantial matters to be an important part of their lives. And, as it quickly became evident, on serious topics, they too had a concordance of view which brought them even closer together.

Thus, at one point after Andrei had been talking of his upbringing in post-Soviet Russia, Beth, remembering her thoughts on Russian history during the flight to Moscow, probed deeper. She asked him for his views on the Bolshevik revolution of 1917, and the new epoch thereby ushered in. In particular, she inquired, "Had it derailed normal development in Russia and, therefore, ultimately retarded the country compared to what would have happened in its absence, or had it ultimately propelled the country forward allowing the possibility of better lives for later generations?"

He had responded very favourably to the question itself, "Yes, this is the key historical question, of much greater relevance than reciting events and moralizing about them individually, which is the usual discourse. Limiting ourselves to individual acts, or even sequences of acts independent of historical context, raises your very own Samuel Johnson's question, 'Who then would escape a whipping?' Context is not everything of course, but it has been close to such in the twentieth century. It has determined what must be done at the macro level, or system wide level, and if leaders did not do what was necessary for the country, they would fall or fail. Since they typically have been men and women of the world, they usually conformed to what was required." Beth was impressed by this agreement on the framing of the matter, as it revealed an understanding of the significance of the macro historical process and implicitly raised the question of what agency people might attain as a consequence.

However, Andrei's substantive answer to her question also did not disappoint. He had continued without much of a pause by saying, "The short version comes down to five points. First, in the early twentieth century some kind of revolution was inevitable in Russia because of its economic and political backwardness, and which threatened the very survival of the country. Moreover, conditions were sufficiently underdeveloped that any revolution would turn out to be very radical. Second, the revolution that actually did occur destroyed much of the old order, but the bulk of what was worth preserving scientifically and culturally was safeguarded and fostered.

Third, while the Soviet regime was brutal, at least for the first forty years, most of the violence occurred in endeavours to secure the country in the event of invasion and promote the economic development required for this. Fourth, this experience was not unique; many countries histories could be characterized in the same way, although perhaps less intensely. Fifth, the collapse of the Soviet Union was not accidental, but it bequeathed a more developed Russia than what would have occurred had it not survived for so long. It, thereby, contributed to people having more comfortable conditions in which to live and also to the possibility of creating more human lives for themselves."

Beth was genuinely swayed because of it dovetailed so closely with her own form of analysis and also her views on Russian history, as well as her general perspective on human affairs. Andrei was clearly as analytical as herself and seemingly also with values not dissimilar to her own. However, she deliberately gave a conventional response in order to probe deeper into Andrei's perspective, "But surely much of Stalin's violence in the collectivization and party purges was gratuitous, was it not?"

Andrei thought for a moment before replying, "It probably was possible for developmental objectives to have been achieved with less violence. However, Stalin is not alone in facing such a charge. Consider, for example, the founding fathers and early presidents of the United States, who preserved slavery and conducted genocidal campaigns against the indigenous peoples in order to develop their country. And also remember modern England's own great leader, Winston Churchill, depriving Bengal of food at the time of famine in 1943 and thereby contributing to millions of Indian deaths because he believed doing so was vital to the war effort of Britain against the Japanese and Germans when it actually was not. Thus, an incredibly significant part of the story in our histories is that circumstances sometimes call for brutes to be in power, and power no doubt brutalizes them even more, so many others suffer excessively. It is not my preference that this be the case, and I believe significant human improvement is possible, but it appears to have been much of the reality of life so far and not just in Russian history. It is about time that people learnt from history and tried to adjust their behaviour accordingly."

"Yes", Beth responded, "I understand and agree wholeheartedly with the main thrust of what you have said, but we are likely somewhat peculiar here. The only other person I know who understands this type of perspective is my friend Charlotte and maybe to a lesser extent her husband, who is my boss in Special Branch. Maybe you are better endowed with friends and colleagues who are on the same wavelength. However, rather than continuing with this topic, much as I would like too, perhaps we should move on to talking of lighter matters before we get really maudlin. After all, we do not have a lot of time left before we must part company." To which, Andrei smiled, nodded, and the conversation moved back into less weighty matters.

The time flew, and as they were sipping their cognac at the end of the meal Beth's telephone rang. It was Charles Ryder, and he launched straight into business. "Great work Beth, and I look forward to seeing you tomorrow. But I have another task for you now. I believe it would greatly help us if Colonel Chekhov could come back to London with you. Given that some of the assassins are Russians, I want him to examine the data base to see if anything suggests itself to him, perhaps raising further questions for Rayevsky. The data base cannot be accessed except from within the Yard. I have checked with General Dorov, and he has no objection to the Colonel helping us further on an open-ended basis, but I also want Chekhov to be on side too so that he will be fully cooperative. Please ask him to accompany you back to the UK and be as persuasive as you possibly can be."

"Will do sir," as she turned to face Andrei with a broad smile on her face.

# V RETHINKING

On the Monday at precisely 11.00 a.m., Charlotte Ryder left the Eurostar express from Paris at King's Cross and St. Pancras station, walked toward the Euston road exit, once again in admiration of the superb fusion between the original and the ultra-modern engineering achieved by the last renovation of the station. But her principal thoughts remained elsewhere. She had just finished a lecture tour of European universities, presenting papers on several topics in political philosophy. Holding a professorship at University College and renowned for her intelligence, she concentrated her research on the analysis of texts held to be classics in her subject. Somewhat analogous to the station, it was a fusion of the old and the new, in this case of older texts and newer intellectual tools provided by Anglo-American analytic philosophy and the more substantive but less rigorous body of continental philosophy. The antiquarian element in her research was also further reduced by the fact that she focused on understanding what was said regarding both the historical specifics and the universals of power in the texts she analyzed. Furthermore, since 'power' was at the very centre of all politics, understanding how the best minds in the subject had understood it throughout the ages meant she regarded herself as being at the forefront of her subject.

The tour had gone well, although she was continually reminded of how the study of politics in universities had changed in recent decades. A substantial section of the professoriate had almost completely jettisoned the study of leading thinkers in the past along with their historical contexts. Instead, they focused on the currently fashionable projects of modern liberalism, such as expanding the role of markets, extending human rights, promoting multiculturalism and deepening the 'global liberal order'. A managerial perspective regarding implementation of these ideals was also prominent in such work. She regarded these issues as including matters of importance, but also as treated typically in the shallowest of fashions that ignored blatant inconsistencies. Classical liberalism, dominant in England between the seventeenth and nineteenth century, had many deficiencies, but it was far more coherent than the modern forms. It had focused on the importance of property rights, constitutional government and the rule of law, which would be insufficient for the needs of today's democratic conditions, but it did not greatly fall foul of logic. Modern liberalism was another matter altogether, lacking a coherent understanding of how human rights can very easily conflict with each other and of why cultures are frequently incompatible. Furthermore, there was no recognition of the fact that stable international orders required a hegemonic power, or a balance of power between the leading states, and as a consequence are fashioned by particularistic interests that made any claimed universality mythical. These properties of human relations might well be unfortunate, particularly for minorities, but it was futile to ignore them or to pretend they did not exist. As for managerialism, its extension into university administration and to the subjects that were taught in universities was an unmitigated disaster. She was reminded once again of the witty remark made by one of her colleagues at University College, "Managerialism came to the universities as the German army came to Poland in 1939 and has had much the same effects."

The problems of modern liberalism as Charlotte saw

them, however, were not simply a result of a deficiency in critical faculties or a misperception of factual matters on the part of those who adhered to the doctrine, and which might, therefore, be susceptible to being corrected through normal debate. Instead, a new orientation centred on what was termed 'moral clarity' had entered the profession and had corroded objective observation as well as rational thought. It assumed that there was one moral position to which all right-thinking people of the 'international community' would ascribe, so the world could be partitioned into a sphere of darkness and a sphere of light with liberals constituting all of the latter. In truth, this was nothing more than self-righteous nonsense. Different systems of power, whether of the past, the present, or potential in the future, embodied different ethics, so the study of politics could never limit itself to a singular moral clarification of issues. Moreover, the pluralism of moralities was not accidental; it was precisely because power needed to be legitimated that different systems of power required different ethics.

However, despite the difference in perspectives, her audiences had usually been polite, albeit appearing not to be especially interested in what she had to say. Sometimes there had been comments dismissive of her subject, but these she positively welcomed because her response could be devastating. Typically, it began with, "We do not call them the classics because they were stupid or marginal, and one dimension of their importance lies in the immense illumination they provide regarding the properties of power, which surely should be of central concern to us. Or is it something else that you and your colleagues' study?" She usually followed with an exposure of the contradictions of the "ever so modern liberalism" that had become fashionable of late but, as she demonstrated with multiple examples, could have no staying power if logic and relevance still had any claim on human intelligence. And, no doubt, the effects of her intellectual response were also reinforced by her striking appearance. She was tall, classically beautiful, with long black hair and an excellent figure, also being invariably smartly dressed and as well-spoken in French and German as she was in English. All in all, she constituted an authoritative presence, and of which she was perfectly aware and did nothing to suppress. But her confidence was without conceit. She realized how lucky she had been in the multiple lotteries of life and her own political allegiances when she was younger had lain squarely on the side of the libertarian left. Now, however, she viewed these ideas as utopian and, therefore, a matter on which it was sensible to remain silent apart from ana-lyzing why they had proved to be so irrelevant or what might revive some parts of them. However, the fact that she was willing to contemplate such matters meant that she understood Beth's political positions, along with hav-ing some considerable sympathy for them.

Naturally, during the previous two weeks of the tour, Charlotte had become out of touch with happenings at home, scarcely getting much beyond what Euronews television and a scanning of the main reports in the Ger-man and French press. But she had hypothesized that her husband was involved in the investigation of the assassin-ations as his telephone calls had been less frequent and the conversations shorter than was usual in recent days. As always, this was a giveaway that he was preoccupied with something profoundly serious and would only con-fide when he saw her in person. And even then, only when he was puzzled and believed she might be of help. She was invariably obliging and knew that her help had often been important once it had been processed by his own critical intelligence, which she recognized as equal to her own. They had met at Cambridge as undergraduates twenty years earlier, fallen in love and had remained devoted whilst managing to have successful careers in quite different areas. Being fortunately unconstrained by lack of financial resources, and less fortunately by the absence of children, they had pursued much of their lives in separate domains, but this had never weakened their commitment to each other.

The taxi journey from the station to her home in Gower Street near to University College was a lengthy one as the demonstrations were continuing, and she was less than pleased when the fare came to over fifty pounds. But she tipped as usual and made no fuss since the driver looked none too pleased with the situation either. Also, as soon as she was out of the cab and not yet in the house, her husband phoned with a loving, albeit brief, welcoming home. He promised to be with her by 6.00 p.m. at the latest and would arrange dinner to be delivered by her favorite Italian restaurant at 7.00 p.m. When he had ended the call shortly thereafter, she hazarded a guess that he would task her with helping the investigation in some way, and thus resolved to do some research. After unpacking and eating lunch, she went to work reviewing many newspaper reports, commentary by columnists, and, especially, the statement of the Committee, while occasionally consulting her own library of books. She reached a conclusion about the ideological character of those behind the assassinations fairly quickly. Indeed, she thought it rather obvious from the Committee's own statement and was surprised that none of the commentators in the press had realized this. There was no need for any deep training in textual analysis to fathom things out, just a serious knowledge of political ideologies. But then she mused once again, university education in Britain on matters concerning politics had been deteriorating for some time and ignorance was evident everywhere. Nonetheless, she did recognize that her conclusion concerning the ideological character of the Committee's statement was somewhat astounding, perhaps even stunning.

***

Charles Ryder arrived home on the dot at 6.00 p.m., embraced Charlotte, and said nothing beyond how much he had missed her, all of which was true as she knew. She had missed him too, acutely, and was ecstatic to be reunited, although far too controlled to be overly demonstrative, as he was. Then they chatted for half an hour mainly about her lecture tour before he broached the subject of the assassinations and his commanding role.

He explained that while the investigation had been very lucky in finding the identity of some of the assassins and in gaining the cooperation of the Russians who had arrested one of them, they had no idea as to who had hired them to undertake their tasks and for what purpose. His team had discussed the matter and opinions were scatter shot. There were those favouring Islamists, others thought the IRA could be involved, and yet some who considered it worthwhile to investigate Trotskyists. But the case for each was never convincing at all, and he as well as Beth were agnostics; they simply did not feel confident enough even to hazard a guess. Could Charlotte do any better? He particularly wanted to know for what purposes the murders had been carried out, and as to whether she could form an opinion as to what political allegiance the organizers had, along with the overall plan of their actions.

"You don't want much do you," she exclaimed, followed by a broad smile and then more seriously, "Yes, I think I can help you, but only in the broadest of terms, and you must be patient while I explain my conjectures. I will do so after dinner when you are somewhat lubricated by the Chianti and more able to experience a shock because what I will say is likely to be very shocking for you."

***

They returned to the matter an hour later. She spoke for around twenty minutes with Charles hanging on her every word, only occasionally interrupting to ask for elucidation. When she had finished, she knew that he was impressed, albeit skeptical. However, it became immediately clear that it was the former aspect that prevailed because he responded with an invitation, "I want you to come to the Yard tomorrow morning at 10 a.m. and repeat what you have just told me in front of my detectives. They will all be there because we are all scheduled to have a 'reporting and discussion session' at that time, and it will be exceedingly helpful if you can explain your ideas then. Each and all have detailed knowledge of the particulars in each killing that goes well beyond what has been released to the press. The only real 'generalists' will be myself and Colonel Andrei Chekhov who is with us on secondment from the FSB in Moscow. He speaks perfect English, is obviously highly intelligent, and he has access to information sources we can only guess at. I propose that you speak as you have to me and then respond to questions and comments. What you have said is so insightful and important; it could constitute another break we so desperately need."

She understood the seriousness of this and responded with an, "Understood Commander," coupled to a mock salute.

***

The Commander called the meeting to order at 10 a.m. the following day, introduced his wife to the detectives and the detectives to her, and explained what she was about to do. He admitted that this was a highly irregular procedure of bringing in an outsider to Special Branch investigations, but it was certainly no less strange than having 'inputs' from the FSB that had proved so productive. "Moreover", he continued, "the investigation needed whatever help it could get," and reinforced this by quoting the Prime Minister's remit to him, "you may do whatever is necessary to solve these crimes." Then without further ado, he passed the meeting over to Charlotte but requested that she not be interrupted as there would be time for questions at the end of her presentation.

Charlotte stood up, went to a lectern, and began immediately, "My subject is political theory, and part of the methods I use are the tools of textual analysis to understand political writings, including in terms of the historical contexts in which they were produced, as well as their relevance more widely. Insofar as I can make any contribution to comprehending the assassinations, it is here. I will concentrate on the Committee's statement released to the news agencies, interpreting it as a political declaration from a particular theoretical perspective in the specific context of contemporary Britain. I hasten to add that I do not myself adhere to the political position I identify as the source of the assassinations. I am only presenting the position in the strongest terms that are possible in order to make the case as convincing as it can be made. I will also speak in an authoritative and academic manner which reflects my occupation, but I readily admit that the argument I will make is not wholly conclusive. It is more in the way of being a 'best guess' in the light of the textual evidence. However, I do believe that it is a particularly good guess, and, hopefully, your questions and comments at the end will shed more light on identifying the organizers of the killings. It has always been my experience that a dialectic of contrary positions is a path to truth so I would encourage you all not to be shy in responding to what I say. I, in turn, promise not to be reticent in my responses. I will speak slowly and with a large number of extended pauses because what I am about to say may be unfamiliar to some of you, and this will allow you all time to write notes for your questions."

Charlotte stopped momentarily before continuing, "The Committee's statement includes three main matters of interest: a diagnosis of problems in British society, what needs to be done to treat them, and a calling for the public's support. There are, of course, more than these matters mentioned, but it is these three that allow me to contribute to understanding the political or ideological identity of the Committee's members. I also will be somewhat repetitive in my explanations because the ideas expressed can be understood better if they are presented in multiple ways. Since there will be time for questions when I am finished, I can also then elaborate further on any issues if necessary."

Charlotte paused, took a sip of water and then launched into her principal claim, "The central point I will argue for is that the diagnosis of the problems of British society are expressed in *conservative* terms, which are quite distinct from those of other political dispositions. By this I mean not what may be widely understood as 'conservative', but what is understood as British conservatism in political theory. In particular, it reflects the conservatism of Edmund Burke, an Anglo-Irish parliamentarian in the late eighteenth century who was prompted to express his views on the nature of socio-political organization and much else by the outbreak of radical revolution in France. Since then he has been regarded as *the* theorist of conservatism in the English-speaking countries of the West and not just by those with an allegiance to conservatism but by political theorists of all persuasions. Of course, there have been changes in conservatism since Burke's day, and many who actually call themselves conservative would be better described as liberals and are quite different from

Burkeans, a point to which I will return in a moment. However, Burkean ideas remain the dominant strand in intellectual conservatism and conservatives who still take ideas seriously recognize this. Not, of course, in the sense of adhering to the specific policy positions that Burke himself favoured over two centuries ago, but in accepting the general principles he expressed as to what was required to ensure a well-functioning society."

She paused again before resuming, "The Burkean view of capitalism, liberal rights and representative government was and remains that they could function properly only if there were strong and appropriately structured social bonds that condition people's behaviour suitably. Everything depends on the quality of the social relationships in the family, local communities, and the associations of civil society, as well as the cultures with which they are joined. Humans are seen as social creatures, and at their best when they inhabit structures of relationships and cultures of belief that form them into unities. This requires the development of overlapping loyalties, whilst simultaneously facilitating the formation of genuine individuals with specific rights and duties within these structures and cultures."

She rested briefly and then recommenced, "What I have said so far is quite abstract, so let me be more concrete to make matters clearer. There are different varieties of conservatism, and I am concentrating on the Burkean version that has been the dominant form in Britain for most of the last two hundred years. I will continue to do so by emphasizing those Burkean elements exemplified in the statement of the Committee and explain them in a way that relates to Burkean concerns. A crucial point is that Burkean conservatives are quite different from 'liberals' in the classical sense. They do not regard people simply as autonomous beings with natural rights and capacities who relate to each other primarily through market exchange. Instead, they regard individuals as being significantly formed by the social relationships in which they participate. Moreover, these relationships of the family, local community, occupational and professional associations of civil society, and the nation state also discipline behaviour. Ideally, self-interests are thereby constrained and channeled into conduct that is seen to be legitimate and trusted by others, thus bringing about cooperative and beneficially productive outcomes for all concerned".

Charlotte took a sip of water before explaining the matter in an alternative manner, "Another way of saying this is to recognize that the Burkean perspective may be defined in terms of the trio: 'station, obligation, nation'. People are formed to hold stations, or positions, in life, which come with benefits and obligations to act appropriately, so aiding others in society as well as themselves. Liberals see part of this when they depict people acting in terms of incentives. But Burkeans would argue that without being embedded appropriately in social relations that inculcate the duties of positions along with the rights, this acting according to incentives will lead to opportunistic behaviour. The result will be less productive and less civilized outcomes because obligations for honest dealing will be avoided whenever possible. It is, therefore, desirable for the political authority to encourage those properties of families, communities, occupational and professional associations, and the legal system to promote the recognition of obligations, honesty and trust in human interactions."

Yet again Charlotte paused before reformulating what had just been said so as to further clarify her argument, "This means that the orientation of Burkean conservatives overlap to some extent with classical liberalism and also classical socialism. In fact, it can be viewed as a distinct complex involving elements of both. Burkean conservatives recognize with liberals that individuals have rights and are acquisitive, but, unlike liberals, they believe these rights need to be buttressed with social obligations to act honestly and deal fairly in carrying out the social roles occupied so acquisitiveness is constrained. Regarding socialism, Burkeans accept that people are socially formed rather than simply autonomous individuals, but, unlike socialists, they do not believe that this implies the desirability of complete equality and socialized property. They argue instead that societies are naturally hierarchical because they require authority structures to operate and persist, and they also need to allow space for some degree of private acquisitiveness because it can result in beneficial outcomes for individuals and society."

"History is also important for Burkeans," Charlotte continued with a change of tack, "they claim that at their most effective the relationships, rights and duties a society exhibits are the heritage of past practices and learning. Thereby, they become infused with an inheritance of historical wisdom as a result of a 'trial and error' adjustment process, sometimes expressed in more elevated terms by referring to it as an 'invisible hand'. Of course, this is a phrase first made famous in the late eighteenth century by Adam Smith in the *Wealth of Nations* with regard to the operation of markets. However, it has now been generalized to social processes by some Burkean conservatives, and Burke himself may well have thought in these terms too. This does not imply that contemporary Burkeans are reactionaries, wanting to freeze change or return to an imagined golden age of the past. They now accept modernity, including most aspects of secularism, science, elected government, the formal equality of all citizens as well as the rule of law. But they do emphasize that each of these matters is an outcome of *particular* historical processes and are not the result of the application of abstract reason favoured by liberals. As Burke himself put the matter, ideally societies and their cultures are associations of generations and thereby constitute a partnership 'not only between those who are living, but between those who are living, those who are dead, and those who are to be born'. There is a 'We', not just an aggregation of 'I's', and policies should nurture this by ensuring that individuals are educated and socialized appropriately to bring about a high degree of continuity."

Now Charlotte stopped speaking for slightly longer to let this new dimension of conservatism sink in and then extended the ideas, "Over time, of course, change would occur, but it was incumbent upon political leaders to safeguard as far as was possible that the change ran along established tracks and did not constitute a radical breach with what previously prevailed. Only then could the social body remain healthy and disruptive change, which would lack any anchor of civilization and was bound to end in disorder, be contained. Nonetheless, it is the case that conservatives can act in ways that appear radical when they believe that there has been a fundamentally important deterioration in circumstances, but they would themselves characterize their actions as 'restorative' in conditions that have seriously departed from a conservative path of change."

Again, Charlotte paused to allow all this to register before resuming, "Burkean Conservatives see all this as remaining essentially true today as in the late eighteenth century and allowing them to recognize major pathologies in British society, including what they regard as the atomization of individuals and the corruption of culture. Most importantly, businessmen have increasingly been given a free hand to operate their enterprises as they alone see fit without sufficient constraints placed upon them to keep within the parameters required for social stability. The powers of countervailing and protective organizations of professional and occupational associations, unions, local communities, and government regulatory agencies have been significantly weakened. This is most obvious in the case of finance and the serious crises that have struck repeatedly, with the most destructive being those of September 2008 and of two months ago. And, in both cases it is precisely those who caused the problems who have been protected by the state's legal, monetary, and fiscal authorities. All others have been left to fend for themselves in circumstances of increasing unemployment, collapsing asset prices and declining incomes. Socialists typically describe or explain all this in terms of the adoption of the policies of 'neoliberalism', 'globalization' and 'financialization' by governments, and while Burkean conservatives would be exceedingly unlikely to use this terminology, they would generally concur with many of the thoughts behind the concepts.

Charlotte now began to address yet another dimension that would shed further light on conservatism, "More generally, from the mid-1970s, the British Conservative party and the British Labour party have both become more classically liberal. There has been greater stress placed on rights, property ownership, and market relations, with lesser emphasis on the importance of duties to others including future generations, the 'mixed economy' and social supports to ensure honest dealing between people. Thus, for example, Harold Macmillan famously described Margaret Thatcher's privatizations as analogous to 'selling the family silver' and, thereby, depriving future generations of their due from those of the past. As a result, Burkeans would certainly accept that capitalism has been significantly unmoored and deregulated, leading to 'moral hazard' in which self-interest is often unaligned with societal interests. In particular, many elites have become egotistical and ignorant of their origins. Rather than acting with a reverence and a sense of gratitude to the nation that formed them and nourished them, they have become radical individualists. This has been facilitated by the development of liberalism in which a wide array of particularistic rights, not always consistent with other rights, are demanded and exercised against the wider society. Simultaneously, representative government has been undermined by globalization and the increasing powers of supra-national organizations. Another way of describing the situation as Burkean conservatives would see it is to say that the atomization of individuals has reached a point of displaying *anomie* in which no generally accepted codes of behavior prevail. Traditions of conformity and integration have broken down because they have lost their authority, and much of this is due to the excessive expansion of the market on a global scale and, again, also to the collapse of intermediate groupings lying between the individual and the state. For the Burkean, such socially isolated individuals are 'lost'; they have no cultural or moral anchors, and all manner of what is sometimes called 'anti-social' behavior occurs, but which actually speaks to the fact that the 'social' has been weakened."

Now Charlotte began her conclusion, "We see all these sentiments clearly expressed in the Committee's statement and no expressions of alternative political orientations, so I would conclude that the statement has been written by conservatives, strange as it may seem to say so. But there is, finally, just one more point I wish to make. The Committee, whoever they are, must believe that the situation of economic and societal fraying, along with the disfunctions they generate, have got to a desperate point, and brought about a situation whereby extreme means have to be employed to engender repair and recovery through the actions of the British government and public. After all, Burkean conservatives, typically, emphasize the importance of order, have a suspicion of the politics of the street and are outright hostile to radicalism. So those behind the assassinations and statement must be convinced that the dissolution of appropriate social relations in British society has reached a dangerous stage. For want of a better term, then, one might refer to the strategy as one of 'conservative radicalism' or 'restorative reaction' and as such reflects a despairing consciousness. However, I do not know who these people actually are as individuals, and I have only presented the case they would make for what they did in the most compelling terms. I have done this, not because I agree with their actions or their beliefs, but because I want to identify them most accurately in political terms in order to help your investigation."

The Commander stood up, thanked Charlotte, and asked for questions or comments from the audience of detectives, with a plea for them not to feel shy about raising queries and objections. It was imperative that the investigation identify the organizers of the killings and given the absence of alternatives the only way was by honing in on them through analysis and discussion of the evidence available.

The first question came quickly from Harry Brown who headed the investigation into the Billy Jones killing, and who was characteristically brusque, "Thank you for your analysis, but I beg to differ. Old-fashioned conservatives with which I am familiar are cuddly-fuddy-duddies in practice, not the efficient killers whose work we are investigating. It must be some other grouping. I do not know who they are, but they cannot be conservatives as I understand the term."

Charlotte's response was pointed and yielded nothing, "Burkeans do not consider themselves old-fashioned and while they can give off the appearances you claim, typically they also have intelligence and a hard edge and can be innovative as well as decisive. Do not confuse the popular stereotype portrayed in Monty Python comedy with the real thing. Think instead, for example, of Winston Churchill in 1940. Remember the morally inspiring language of nation in which he spoke to the British people as well as the ruthlessness with which he sought to maintain the empire and prosecuted the war."

John Simmons, who led the investigation of the Rory Candiman killing, was the next to raise doubts along similar lines but was more substantive in formulating his disagreement, "I think it much more likely that a terrorist group lies behind the killings. After all, the *modus operandi* is terrorist is it not? And the Committee's statement describes the violent actions taken as terroristic!"

Charlotte's rejoinder was quite devastating as she had expected such a reaction given recent history and had also taken note of the references to terrorism in the Committee's statement, "As far as we can gather, the intended targets were dispatched, and no one else were killed or injured. The Committee's statement makes a point of this too. Indeed, it appears that those killed were carefully chosen, and serious measures were taken to ensure there was no collateral damage. This behavior is in marked contrast to terrorists as commonly understood today who do not precisely differentiate, and for whom it is all to the good if casualties are maximized. Indeed, one might say that the central characteristic of modern terrorist acts is the murder of innocents. Furthermore, why would any of the terrorist groups we know of make the particular demands made in the Committee's statement? And, if you look, you will see that much of the populace of London are in the streets demonstrating their support, which they certainly would not do if they believed the usual type of terrorist cells were the active force behind the killings. To properly understand the reference to terrorism in the Committee's statement, one must recognize what the term used to mean in past and which could be assumed as long gone until the actions of the Committee revived it. I mean by this, terrorism which is directed at the privileged and powerful who are supportive of the regime that prevails and is, therefore, quite the contrary to what the term means today. Thus, this usage of the term in the Committee's statement actually supports my contention that it is Burkeans who are its source."

Eric Fowler, heading the investigation into the killing of James Stewart, was more measured and less confrontational, first making an observation and then raising a query rather than stating an explicit counter, "I understand that you are dissecting the Committee's statement in order to locate the authors and, by implication, the assassin's identity. But what if there is a false trail being laid? What if the aim of the killers in writing the statement was to confuse, thereby aiding in the concealment of the real identity of the organizers of the crimes by throwing us off the scent? John's point is not so easily dismissed if this is borne in mind."

Charlotte's answer, too, was more measured than that of her previous two responses, but she did not lack a powerful retort, "Yes, I understand the logic of what you say. But, and it is a big 'but', modern terrorists typically do not want to confuse in this way because they are proud of their 'achievements' and use them as recruiting tools among other things, so they want their political identity known. In addition, most if not all of the groups and people we call terrorists are likely pretty ignorant of Burkean conservatism. Hence, they would lack the capacity to articulate its thoughts and sentiments in the way that the Committee's statement clearly does. Moreover, the authors of the statement call on the British people to act and demonstrate their support for conservative measures, not for anything that terrorists of the usual variety would be interested in."

Eric was far from pleased by this answer. He recognized its validity, and this was the problem. Not only was his ego offended; more importantly, he judged it likely that Beth would not be impressed at all by what he had said. Indeed, he thought the matter had probably detracted from any respect she may have had for him. This made him even more depressed and unhappy as she had recently become the very centre of his romantic ambitions.

Gordon Sinclair, in charge of the Stephanie Almiston case, followed and was considerably more cerebral, "I take your point that the identities of the organizers of the assassinations are unlikely to be terrorists. But there is an alternative reading of the Committee's statement to the one you have given. The hostility to elites suggests a populist grouping is involved. After all, the claim that elites act contrary to the interests of the vast majority of people is at the heart of all populisms. Should we not then look to those populist groups who are presently active in the country?"

Charlotte recognized the intelligence of this question and began with an endorsement yet yielded nothing of substance, "You have pointed to a significant quality in the Committee's statement. But it does not contradict anything I have said, rather it reinforces it. This may not appear to be the case because all conservatives are elitists while the Committee is clearly hostile to presently dominant elites in Britain. However, as Burkeans, the Committee members favour only particular types of elites whose characteristics I have outlined. Moreover, they believe that the elites they favour have been pushed aside by new types that are bringing wrack and ruin to the country and must, therefore, be replaced. In other words, conservatives, as I have described them, can appear to be populists because they are not blind supporters of elites or the privileged in all circumstances and can both criticize and seek to discipline them severely. In their view, elites have functions to perform, and they can be exercised well or poorly. In the latter case, conservatives would recognize the need for remedial action. Moreover, conservatives are well aware of what is sometimes referred to as the 'cultural contradictions of capitalism', whereby acquisitiveness becomes egoistic and corrodes the economic performance of the system along with the historical legacy it once incorporated. It does so by encouraging monopolies, predation and cheating to the point of criminality, so encouraging a populist response. And the Committee's statement actually calls for such because they are with the people in believing that capitalism must be re-embedded in the social, moral and legal orders that ensure appropriate behaviours. In other words, conservatism, as I understand it and have described it, is not concerned solely with defending 'what is'. The core value for them is the defence of a well-functioning way of life in which all have a place, or if you prefer the presently fashionable descriptor, 'to promote inclusivity', albeit of a very particular form that recognizes the pivotal role of elites acting in a Burkean manner. Thus, conservatives in the current circumstances can even agree with radical populists that elites need to be restrained, but there is a huge difference in that conservatives actually want the particular types of elites they favour to rule. They are not against elites *per se*. There is also one further point that I should add to further buttress what I have argued. Actual populists do not write in the manner of conservatives and do not know how to write in this way. Indeed, they are frequently hostile to all conservatives because they wrongly see them as unconditional supporters of all elite practices."

Gordon did not seem fully satisfied with this response to his question, but he did not follow up with a rejoinder, and there was an extended pause before Beth finally punctured the silence with a comment and observation, "I accept what you have said in your analysis Charlotte, both in your presentation and in your responses to questions by my colleagues, but there really is a puzzle here which you have so far not addressed, although it was clearly alluded to by Harry in his question. Conservatives of an intellectual disposition in the manner you have presented them may have had the motive to kill as they did and to propose a public response as they did, but how did they come by the means? The assassinations were highly sophisticated violent acts exhibiting a wide range of competencies. These are not generally associated with the type of conservative to which you refer, especially in peacetime and in their own society, and nor is the knowledge necessary to access the services of professional assassins."

Charlotte's reaction this time was altogether different than it had been hitherto, but it was also accompanied by another shocking deduction, "You make excellent points, but conservatives are everywhere still located in the upper echelons of the British state. They are not just parliamentarians, local party secretaries, academics, journalists and independent intellectuals. While they are far fewer in number and have much less influence over policy than they did forty or so years ago, they retain a presence with a particular set of dispositions that I have sought to outline either inside, or associated with, the governmental apparatus. It is on the organs of power you need to focus!"

Andrei Chekhov stood up and followed on immediately, "Your analysis is impressive professor. As a member of the leading Russian intelligence service, I have been well-educated in the sharp end of British security policies over many decades, some of them formulated by government ministers and civil servants who appear to have been conservatives in the sense of the description you provide. Naturally, I cannot go into details, but I do believe you are on the right track, and your thesis is the best we have available at present. British conservatism can be ruthless when it is recognized as imperative to be so, and this has typically been coupled to intelligent implementation. I also believe that what you have said also contributes to answering the question of why 'these five and not others' were killed. Given the purpose as you analyze it, the specific individuals did not matter profoundly. Another set, who engaged in similar practices and could, therefore, be seen as similarly degenerate, would have done just as well. And this is fully consistent with what Rayevsky told us about the instructions of no innocents being harmed. The Committee may well have had substitute assassinations in their back-up plans if there was to be collateral damage in those chosen to be the five who died and which thus warranted cancellation."

Charlotte did not respond other than nodding her head in acknowledgement and appreciation.

The Commander then intervened, "If Charlotte and Andrei are correct, we should be looking for a group within the agencies of state and, moreover, ones with violent capabilities that exist in-house or know how they can be hired from the ranks of professional assassins. I would guess that this means a grouping within the armed forces, or the police, or the security services," ending on a rare humourous note, "I think we can ignore the Department of Pensions and such like."

At which point, Beth spoke once again, "How do we find out from whence they came?" immediately answering the question herself. "Our best guess can only be to assume some unit gone rogue, and perhaps the most sensible strategy is to bring the Prime Minister or the Cabinet Secretary into our deliberations and ask for guidance. Surely, they must have wider sources of information than we do."

There was a general nodding all-round the room, indicating that there was at least a rough convergence of opinion regarding the need to follow up on the logic of Charlotte's analysis even if some serious doubts remained of its validity.

***

At 2.00 p.m., the Commander entered the room of Sir Richard Armitage, in the complex that actually constituted 10 Downing Street. The Prime Minister was in Brussels dealing again with an assortment of matters connected to the relationship of the UK with the European Union. So, it was to Sir Richard that Ryder turned, and he was more than happy to do as there was little about the British state apparatus that he was ignorant of. And, unsurprisingly, he was highly intelligent, typically calm, collected and disciplined. Usually, he was also charming, but also he had a well-deserved reputation for doing whatever was necessary when circumstances called for such. In addition, and equally unsurprising, he was always smartly dressed, cultivated in taste and highly presentable in appearance. He was in his mid-sixties with greying hair, slightly above average height, and looked younger than his actual years, all of which induced a commanding presence and authoritative voice for those privileged to receive his views.

The Commander explained the course of the investigation, and the conclusions reached so far in the investigation at some length, ending with the hypothesis that it was a rogue element in the security services, the armed forces or the police from which the attacks came and that their political orientation was likely that of traditional conservatism. The Commander then played the tape of his wife's presentation of her analysis. Sir Richard listed intently, making some notes as he did so. When the tape had finished, the Commander commented, "Maybe this is a slender reed, but it is really the only reed we have as to who was ultimately behind the assassinations."

Sir Richard responded, "I do not think it so slender Commander. Indeed, I am distressed to say that I find what your wife says highly persuasive as I have been thinking along not dissimilar lines, albeit ones that have been far less well-defined than those she elucidates. It had been my conjecture that the organizers of the assassinations were neither terrorists in the conventional sense or functionaries of a foreign intelligence agency, but that they were very much home-grown. It was this conclusion that led me to recommend to the Prime Minister that Special Branch, and not the security services have responsibility for the investigation, and he quickly accepted this as he had his own deeper and more serious reservations about MI5 and MI6, some of which I also share but which I cannot elucidate to you. It has also probably not escaped your notice that I myself lean toward a traditional conservatism and am a great admirer of Burke, and this gives me a basis for understanding the actions you are investigating in the same way as your wife. I found her characterization of the motives behind the assassinations astute and compelling. Her understanding of the genuinely conservative critique of contemporary Britain is spot on. She is exceptionally clever, and we are lucky that she was available to the investigation. It is also heartening that such intelligence still populates our universities. There is no substitute for competence and genuine knowledge. However, while I understand the logic of what she says, have no fear that I am anything other than appalled by what has happened and determined to locate those responsible. We, the British, must solve are problems in a more civilized manner. I also accept the logic of your conclusion that there could well be a rogue element in the organizations of the state, and, I think, I may be able to help you identifying where it may be. Please continue to be so good and not interrupt me; you can respond when I have finished."

Sir Richard continued, "My view is that it is unlikely to actually inhabit the police, or MI5 and MI6, or the armed forces, although those responsible for the assassinations may have some form of association with people in these organizations. The controls we have in place are simply too strong to allow the formation of the kind of grouping required to carry out such complex activities as the five assassinations from within the organizations themselves, and you will know part of this yourself from being in Special Branch. However, that does not end the matter. You will not be aware, at least I hope you are not aware, as this would be a breach of established secrecies, that there is a unofficial, one might almost say clandestine, grouping of notables who organize operations that would not be suitable for the official security services, the police or the armed forces. And, hopefully, their very existence is not known to the official agencies; although, I cannot guarantee this since MI5 and MI6 now have extraordinary capabilities, and I have long suspected that the notables have had close relations, perhaps far too close relations, with leading members of these organizations, so they may be less secure than generally presumed. This, too, factored into the PM's assignment of the investigation to Special Branch and my concurrence with that decision. As a consequence, I do not want you to contact members of the security services on this matter as they may well be in two minds about aiding you. Moreover, I know all the details you will require to continue your investigation. In a way, I hope nothing comes of it, but from what you have told me,

I am also prepared to face the fact that my hopes will be dashed. So, I will give you the particulars that you need, on the understanding that you keep me completely informed of any conclusions you come too before proceeding to the next stage if it transpires that such a stage becomes necessary. I, myself, have never been supportive of the existence of this grouping of notables. While I do understand that it has been useful, I have also always thought it to be a possible threat if it goes rogue in any way. It had not occurred to me prior to this meeting with you that this possibility had become a probability, but what you have said and particularly your wife's analysis has certainly stoked my old fears."

The Cabinet Secretary then excused himself and said he would be back shortly when he would provide the requisite information. Which he did twenty minutes later, handing Charles a single sheet of paper listing five names and the positions they held in various organizations along with their home addresses, all in his own handwriting.

*Sir Lawrence Forrester, Managing Director, Forrester, Middleton, and Grieve Investments, The City, and 1 Turlie Place, Marlebourne. James Grieve, A partner in the bank above, but holding no executive position. 16 Palin Street, Hampstead. Sir Robert Middleton, A partner in the bank above, and Director of "London Events" for the Home Counties Association, and 2 Ormand Street, Chelsie. Fraser Elliot, Arts and Culture Director, Artful Productions, and 21 Furlough Gardens, South Kensington. Charles Olivier, Duke of Linechester, Acting Head of City Galleries, and 3 Abington Road, St. John's Wood.*

Sir Richard added, "Please use this information wisely and make sure that those you tell it to do so as well.

And keep me updated. You have all my contact numbers and can use them at any time, day or night."

Since the Commander had no questions and was elated at the reception and response he had received, the meeting ended shortly thereafter. And, on returning to the Yard, the Commander reported the contents of his meeting, once again swearing all to absolute secrecy. He then delegated his detectives to find out as much as possible on "the five", and to do so without liaison with any other organizations or personnel outside Special Branch. He divided up the tasks to his detectives, emphasizing again and again the sensitive nature of what they were about to do. The only one present who was left with no task was Andrei. As the meeting ended, however, the Colonel asked the Commander if he could speak to him in private, and they immediately went to Charles Ryder's office, the door was shut, and the Commander smiled with the words, "You have my complete attention, Andrei."

He immediately began to speak very definitely, "Your ultra-secret service may not be so secret after all. In particular, the FSB may know of them, and, if they do, they will monitor communications as best they can, and their best is rather good. No doubt MI5 and MI6 are too, but we are not allowed to use them. Thus, while I know this will go against the grain somewhat, I believe we should use the resources of the FSB instead. We have Rayevsky in custody in Moscow, and he has provided details of his many telephone numbers and bank accounts along with what he knows about the other killers. We could not use some of this information because of the restrictions placed on the investigation with regard to accessing the services of MI5 and MI6 and, therefore, of the Government Communications Headquarters (GCHQ). And since we did not have any definite suspects, we could not have known what to look for exactly. Now, however, we believe we know the members of the Committee, so any communications and money transfers from them to Rayevsky and the other assassins can in principle be found. They may already be in the data banks of the FSB and assuming the FSB remains in a cooperative disposition, as I believe they do, we can get hold of information that is capable of proving that our conjectures are correct. Do you want me to go to the Russian Embassy and make the relevant inquiries?"

The Commander could hardly believe his ears, but not because of the idea of using the FSB shocked him; it was because he had not thought of the same possibility himself. He now realized that given the huge restrictions placed on the investigation, it was a staggeringly obvious route to take. "Of course," he replied, "please do so as rapidly as possible. You and the FSB have been enormously helpful to us so far. Consequently, despite the unusual nature of our cooperation, I have every confidence that this is a productive channel to work along. It is immensely intelligent for you to suggest it, and I am just kicking myself for not having thought of it too. I will order a car to take you to the Russian Embassy in Kensington Palace Gardens. Please get back to me regarding any findings as quickly as you can, whether day or night. You have all my contact numbers."

# VI RESOLUTION

The Commander, the five senior detectives and Colonel Chekhov met at the Yard early the next morning. Charles Ryder reported on his decision the previous afternoon to allow Andrei to try to gain confirmatory evidence on the names provided by the Cabinet Secretary through the use of the FSB surveillance capacities. He admitted that this was highly unorthodox but since the investigation had been ordered not to use the services of MI5 and MI6, along, therefore, with those of GCHQ, there was no other avenue to follow. Moreover, he had been given *carte blanche* to do what was necessary by the Prime Minister himself and had thus enthusiastically agreed to the suggestion by Andrei to seek information from Russian intelligence. Charles Ryder then passed the meeting over to Andrei so that he could report on the findings he had conveyed to him two hours earlier, adding as he always did that there would be time for questions when Andrei had finished so, as usual, the instruction was not to interrupt while the findings were presented.

Andrei went straight to the point, "There is good news. The assassinations can be linked to the Committee, directly in the case of Sir Lawrence Forrester of the Forrester, Middleton and Grieve Bank, and indirectly to the other four names we have through his communications to them. The details of what the FSB analysts found are as follows. The phone call made by Nikolay Rayevsky to report the successful assassination of Sir Roger Gilchrest was made on an unregistered phone, sometimes referred to as a burner phone, to another unregistered phone, as was to be expected. But Rayevsky was able to provide us with the number of the phone he used and the number that he called, as well as the approximate time at which the communication took place. Rayevsky has an excellent memory, as I can attest from my dealings with him, and also every incentive to tell the truth as you all know because of his agreement with the FSB. Moreover, the FSB has been able to confirm that the call was received within the FMG bank, whose head is Lawrence Forrester, and he is the first on the list of names provided by the Cabinet Secretary yesterday. The FSB was also able to confirm that there were four further calls to the same phone number in the bank from locations close to where the four other assassinations occurred. This was achieved through triangulation, and all the calls conform to the times one would expect from the information we already have on the assassinations. In addition, the FSB were able to locate telephone calls made from within the FMG bank from a different unregistered phone to four other phones, also unregistered, that were received in areas consistent with what could be expected to be the locations of the other four Committee members from the information provided by the Cabinet Secretary and at times close to the confirmation of the assassinations. Again, this was achieved through triangulation. Moreover, the contents of the phone calls are all reaffirming evidence. I have transcripts available for your perusal, if you wish, and while the conversations are brief and coded, they are not difficult to decipher as pertaining to the assassinations in the light of what we already know."

Andrei paused for a moment before continuing, "Furthermore, shortly after the assassination of Sir Roger Gilchrest had been confirmed, a transfer of fifty thousand US dollars was made from an account in the FMG bank to one of Rayevsky's bank accounts, which, Andrei smiled, he was good enough to provide us with information upon. Also, at times close to those when the other assassinations were confirmed, a further four payments were made of $30,000 each to four other accounts. Rayevsky was able to verify that one of these payments was to an account he knew to be used by Vladimir Romanovitch and Ernst Schneideral, the assassins of Billy Jones, but he was unable to provide any information on the other account holders. Nonetheless, Rayevsky did think that the amounts involved were a 'fair price', as he so eloquently put it, for the work undertaken. I should also add that tracing these financial transfers was somewhat more complicated than it might seem as there was considerable zigzagging of the monies through various accounts in different banks before their end points. They were indeed similar to modern supply chains of the neoliberalized global economy. However, the technicians at the FSB are confident that they located the trails correctly and, in my experience, they are very competent people. All in all, I believe that the evidence is such that we have all the Committee members conclusively involved in all the killings." And with that he sat down thankful for the rest after a night of no sleep.

The Commander thanked Andrei and commented that he now believed there to be sufficient evidence to arrest all those on the list provided by Sir Richard, but he recognized it best to allow questions for a short period before organizing the arrests as he wanted everyone on board with subsequent actions. With that he opened up the meeting, and Beth was the first to raise her hand with question for Andrei, "Everything you have said is enormously impressive, but why was bitcoin not used in the payment of the assassins. This would appear to have been the obvious way to ensure that no financial trail was available for anyone to find."

Andrei stood up and his response was without hesitation, "I asked the very same question and received elucidation after a further interrogation of Rayevsky. Apparently, professional assassins increasingly look upon themselves as businessmen and businesswomen, with definite costs for each operation and, therefore, having the need for definite revenue to ensure a profit. Given the huge fluctuations in the values of bitcoin in actual currencies, it is not favoured as a method of payment. The preference is for American dollars. As Rayevsky put the matter, 'It was the currency used for virtually all international transactions, and at least some of the assassinations were such'. I also checked with two specialists in the FSB, and they confirmed that all this is highly likely true since from what we know at least a few of the assassins were not residents of the UK".

John Simmons then intervened with an extended comment, "What Andrei has reported is not only impressive and definitive, it also fits the emerging narrative of the investigation. Professor Ryder provided an account of the motives that appeared to prompt the assassinations. Andrei has just illuminated the connection to the means employed, and my colleagues and I have just recently unearthed the expression of conservative views and sentiments by all five names provided by Sir Richard. These were often in obscure political journals, but they certainly support the coherence of the chronicle as a whole. So, we now have compelling evidence on motive and means and can be certain that the perpetrators of the crimes are who we think they are."

All the detectives and Andrei nodded, while the Commander said, "Yes John, you put it very well. We do have compelling evidence that fits together in a coherent story. I have no doubt that we know for certain who the guilty parties are."

Beth responded immediately, "I agree completely,

but we still have a puzzle to solve. In using an unregistered phone inside the bank, Forrester was taking a huge risk that British security services would put two and two together and deduce something similar to what we have done. After all, GCHQ monitors all communications in the UK and, while they would lack the information Rayevsky provided us, there would probably be enough to bring at least some of the Committee members under suspicion. Why have they been so sloppy or silent?"

The Commander stood up and spoke very deliberately. "All of you have no doubt been aware that the Prime Minister and the Cabinet Secretary have something against the security services of MI5 and MI6, and indeed they do. From what I can gather, they have multiple concerns, but the most serious is the belief that the services include people at senior levels that cannot any longer be trusted. They have not made me privy to the details, but from what Beth has just said it would appear that the concerns of the Prime Minister and Cabinet Secretary are not just matters of personal pique or prejudice. Most likely, I would guess, they believe the two services have been captured by American interests and, therefore, cannot be relied on to defend British concerns. This may well include seeking to undermine the Prime Minister himself and his government, which suggests at least turning a blind eye to the activities of the Committee. I am also told that the PM has long had bad personal relations with the heads of both MI5 and MI6 and would like to replace them, but this has not so far proved possible. Likely as not, however, they will be dispatched very soon after we have dealt with the assassinations and the organizations themselves will experience a thorough house cleaning. But, as things stand at present, perhaps the Committee had good reasons not to fear the prying eyes of GCHQ, and deductions made on its basis by the British security services. I do not know, but a 'perhaps' is clearly relevant in the circumstances. And, if anything, it lends support to the results just reported by Andrei."

Harry Brown then raised his hand, "I think the evidence we have from Andrei is pretty conclusive, but as you say sir it has been gathered by most unorthodox means. How can any of it be made to stand up in court?"

The Commander answered without hesitation and again very deliberately, "That is actually not our problem Harry. I have been in touch with Sir Richard, informed him of the results we have from the FSB, and he has approved my requests that arrests be made. Whether anything ever comes to court, and if it does what evidence is presented and with what stage managing is not a matter that need concern us. Much higher authorities will be involved in such decisions, and I very much doubt that there will be any consultation with Special Branch on anything other than a reminder that we are all bound by the official secrets act. Thus, if in the future we read reports in the press of any such trial, we may very well be shocked at the divergence from the reality we know, but we should not be surprised. Given the disturbances and disorder that has been engendered by the actions of the Committee, the authorities will not want to paint them accurately. However, my suspicion is that it will never come to a court case."

Eric Fowler immediately interjected with a critical comment, "What you say Commander is most disturbing. After all, we are police and as such part of a justice system that is the envy of the world. But now it appears we are to be participants in illegitimate activities ourselves."

Ryder responded to this with some delicacy, "I understand your concern Eric, and it is well that you raised it as I am sure you are not alone in feeling a degree of discomfort. But we must also remember two things. First, we are not simply the police; we are Special Branch officers, and, therefore, concerned with matters of state security. Second, as a consequence of the large-scale disturbances and disorder engendered by the actions of the Committee, the government has declared a state of emergency and will consider the whole matter to fall under the Defence of the Realm. It would be a very difficult task to argue conclusively that they are completely wrong in believing this. Consequently, the normal rules of government and of legitimation do not apply. And this fact is reinforced if we consider the unusual nature of this investigation. We have been aided mightily by two outside sources that have nothing to do with those we usually work with. My wife, Charlotte, provided the central clues as to the identity of the perpetrators of the assassinations and Andrei, a Colonel in the FSB no less, provided the crucial evidence that makes us sure we have identified the criminals. However, I have no objection to continuing the discussion of Eric's concerns because I doubt if he is alone in thinking as he does, and we in Special Branch pride ourselves on our incorruptibility. We should, therefore, be sure that what we are doing is the right thing to do in the circumstances we face. For my part, I believe the government is correct in acting as it has done because, as I have just said, the normal rules of legitimation do not apply. As my wife would put the matter, it is a case where 'the political' becomes paramount and takes on a clarification that is generative of extreme measures."

The Commander paused for a moment before continuing, "By this reference to 'the political' she would mean 'the distinction of friend and enemy,' and the 'unusual measures' would be employment of the most effective means to defeat the enemy irrespective of law. As you have experienced, she is a woman of remarkable analytical abilities and of late has been wonted to impress on me that political systems, and the social orders they sustain, are not always on constitutional autopilot. While it is true that in normal times, they seem to be in that the legal structure and institutional practices appear to rule unchallenged, when a threat of substance to the prevailing political and legal order itself does materialize, as in the case we are presently dealing with, so-called 'decisionism' takes over. A state of emergency is declared, and power is less constrained as its reach is both significantly extended and deepened because the overriding objective is the preservation of the order itself."

Again, the Commander paused to let this sink in, and then resumed, "There can be no legal order without sovereign authority to specify the law, interpret the law, and, above all, defend the law. No system of law can sustain itself, and no constitution can be secured by its own rules when it is existentially challenged. In these circumstances a 'state of exception' from law must be enacted as a means of the defence of law. This is the situation we find ourselves in and it is unlikely to end simply with the arrest of the Committee members. The framing and justification of what they have done has proved to be hugely popular as one can see from the continuing demonstrations and disorder, and the powers that be will want some economizing with the truth along with a creative reconstruction so as to discredit the Committee's motives and actions. This does not mean that reforms will not be introduced in order to address manifest discontents once it is clear that the order is secured, but securing the order is the prime imperative at present; such is the logic of 'the political' and 'decisionism' at this juncture".

Harry Brown interjected at this point, remarking, presumably in support of Eric's concern, "All this is very Machiavellian."

Ryder took up the implicit challenge immediately and responded, "Quite so Harry, but while we are within the discourse of political philosophy, and it is supremely relevant given the concern raised by Eric, I should say it is actually more Schmittian than Machiavellian. Again, I have the benefit of my wife's expertise here. She has brought to my attention not only the argument I have just made, but also the terminology used in doing so. References to 'the political' and 'decisionism' come from the writings of Carl Schmitt, a political and legal theorist whose principal work was done during the inter-war years in Germany. He was an unsavory character but is also known for his incisive analytic abilities, and his writings have recently had an influence on political theory generally, including in understanding liberal democracies. This is not because of any sympathy with Schmitt's own substantive political leanings, but rather it stems in large part from a concern with understanding what may be necessary for the preservation of any political system, including our own. He was a Machiavellian, but he also goes beyond Machiavelli and also says things that are unpleasant to hear. However, the issues addressed are matters of truth and appropriate action, not matters pertaining to comfort and contentment. Or, put alternatively, he was himself disreputable, but his thought captures essences of power and legality with a clarity that others cannot rival."

Again, Charles Ryder paused and took a sip of water before continuing, "Schmitt was concerned principally with describing what is true and what must be true of any particular state of affairs, rather than recommending a change to prevailing political arrangements or proposing some political innovation in the support of such a change. This makes what was said relevant for us because we are concerned with what is and what must be in present day Britain. Moreover, it appears that the dominant powers in our government agree with Schmitt. Whether or not they recognize this intellectual heritage or not, and I suspect they do not, is beside the point. The issue is what is necessary to preserve the order within which the government was elected to maintain and nourish. More generally, all political systems have an inside and an outside, and the outside is extra-legal. Or, put more succinctly, 'orders' have mechanisms to maintain themselves in extremis, and we are part and parcel of these mechanisms at the moment."

The Commander paused again before summarizing his argument, "Thus, the most accurate way to define the situation is to say the government has suspended normal, constitutional, legal practices so as to counter a threat to these practices. As such they will employ a range of abnormal procedures to restore normality. There are no grounds for believing that they intend to fundamentally alter the system in the long run. And with the arrest of the Committee and their portrayal as conspirators and revolutionaries seeking radical change by illegitimate means for nefarious purposes, so hopefully quelling popular demonstrations, the government will return the country to normal. And they are most likely sensible enough to know that some reforms addressing the concerns of the Committee and popular discontents will need to be implemented for normal conditions to be fully secured. As a consequence, while we may facilitate a process of falsification, we do so only to guarantee that the conditions in which we can live truthful lives can be reestablished. Put alternatively, peaceful order has typically been supported in multiple ways: by ideologies of the divine, reason, nation, the nature of things, and so forth, but ultimately any order is maintained by 'the political' and 'decisionism'."

Eric nodded but did not concede, "Of course, you are right Commander. The government will probably seek to preserve the central institutional components of the existing order. But we should not ignore the prospect that it will also involve a 'big lie' or 'big lies' in doing so as you, yourself, suggest. And they may not be successful here. There are many people on the streets protesting in favour of the changes proposed in The Committee's Statement of Purpose, and some of the high and mighty of British society appeared to be aligned with them. I think we should be incredibly careful in how we act, if only because we do not know who we will have to answer to in the future."

Harry Brown followed on immediately. "I propose that if any of us object to the framing of the motives of The Committee, along with the treatment they receive after their arrests, we say and act appropriately as we think *then* and not before. There are many avenues for doing so, since the news media will still be functioning, and social media is also a powerful force these days as many governments have experienced to their cost. Thus, I propose that we proceed with the arrests of the members of The Committee. That is clearly the appropriate action to take whatever emerges in the future, and it does not bind any of us to concur with subsequent statements and actions of the government. As a consequence, what any of us do in the face of illegitimate behaviour of the authorities in the future can be a deferred decision; we do not have to decide now, either as a group or as individuals. Instead, we can all postpone decisions beyond what must be done in arresting the members of The Committee. Of course, we should remain alert regarding what the government says and does and prepare to resist in the face of malpractices, but the present is not the time to act in an oppositional way."

There was general agreement from the detectives that this was appropriate, including Eric, although the Commander made no comment. Whether or not they had all fully appreciated the detour into the high theory of the 'political' and 'decisionism' they recognized the common sense of the matter. The claim that the ultimate foundation of the legal order had to lie outside the law appeared to have an indisputable coherence after it had been explained by Charles Ryder, and they each had immense respect for the Commander's and also his wife's analytical abilities, so no further argument occurred. It was also clear to one and all that The Committee members were fully legitimate targets for arrest irrespective of how the government behaved in the future. And, equally clearly, there was relief that any determination of whether or not opposition to the government was appropriate could be postponed.

The Commander, therefore, turned to the practical business at hand, explaining that he wanted the arrests to be carried out simultaneously, so there could be no warnings provided from the Committee members to each other, or, inadvertently, by news organizations who were on the ball with their reports of police actions. He continued, "Consequently, it was imperative to know the location of all five persons prior to the arrests actually being carried out, and to this end I have authorized surveillance teams who will provide continuous updates as to locations of the targets and other relevant information. Whatever there is known about their homes, their usual locations and the places of occupation is also in the process of being accumulated and organized. Everything will be available to you on the data base. While the arrests are being actually carried out, I will stay at the Yard and be contactable by one and all if problems arise."

The Commander then looked at his notes and continued, "I have assigned each of the five senior detectives to the arrest of one member of the Committee. The arrest of Sir Lawrence Forrester has been assigned to John, James Grieve is to be dealt with by Beth, Sir Robert Middleton by Gordon, Fraser Elliot by Harry and Charles Olivier by Eric. Please formulate plans for the arrests by 1.00 p.m. when we will meet again. And in doing so, please be aware that

I have authorized all members of all teams to draw weapons and have fully armed units of police officers on call if they are thought to be needed. In addition, there are two SAS special forces detachments available to us if we need their capabilities. So, unless there any questions, I propose we meet again at 1.00 p.m., and, until then, the time will be devoted to formulating the arrest plans from the information that is being continuously made available regarding photographs, locations, habits and so forth of our targets. I will be here throughout and, as always, can provide clarification, advice and 'what not' to you all. Andrei is going back to his hotel to sleep as he has been up all night. I am sure that we all agree, it will be a well-deserved rest. The quality of the information that he has been able to provide us is without equal."

With that the detectives all stood, looked at Andrei, and clapped.

***

At 1.00 p.m. all the five senior detectives and the Commander met yet again. Each reported on the plan of action as it was by then fairly certain where each of the five targets would be located at 3.05 p.m., the assigned time the plans would be carried out. Only Beth had a serious problem, which she explained succinctly, "James Grieve lives with his cook and servant in a large house in Hampstead, and, if he keeps to his routines, which is to be expected, he will be there all day. However, there is not much information on the layout of the house, and it is unclear exactly how many exits there are and where they are all located, or where they lead too. The house also has extensive gardens front and back, as well as at the sides, and from the aerial shots they all appear to be rather overgrown. So, in short, I think it wise that one of the SAS units available to us be activated. As I understand their capabilities and skills, they would be most suited to dealing with some problems that might arise if the suspect manages to get out of the house into the so-called gardens. I have already spoken to Lieutenant-Colonel Jacobs who heads the larger unit available to us, and he sees no difficulty in the placement of his men and the securing the grounds of the house without arousing suspicion from any one inside the house or the neighbourhood. He understands, of course, that we want Grieve taken alive with all his faculties in working order and again sees no difficulty with these constraints. As a consequence, I would like the Colonel's unit available and in place by 3.05 p.m."

The Commander agreed without hesitation and directed all the detectives to continue with fine-tuning the organizing of the arrests that they had each been assigned.

***

The arrests began simultaneously on the dot of 3.05 p.m., and by 4.30 p.m. all five members of the Committee were in the cells of Special Branch. The Commander and arresting detective visited each in turn, providing all of the arrested with a sheet of paper on which was printed a confession to the crimes with which they had been charged and asked them to study it carefully as they would be requested to sign it the following morning with appropriate witnesses in attendance. No legal counsel would be made available to them at this stage and when counsel was made available, it would not be of their choosing. He recommended that they consider their options very carefully, which he stated clearly to each of the five individually, "I have consulted with the relevant authorities on this matter, and the alternatives you each face are twofold. Confess and cooperate and your fate, while unpleasant, would be mild given the severity of the crimes you have committed. You will be detained at Her Majesty's pleasure, which you will know means detention without trial, in relatively comfortable conditions. By contrast, failure to confess and cooperate would again lead to detention but in conditions that would be far from your tastes, and such that your survival could not be assured. If you use your imagination, I believe you can anticipate what they might be. So, I look forward to your cooperation and will return tomorrow with my companion and also with professional interrogators who will have been fully briefed on what we know of your activities and will want to understand all of the details."

When the Commander addressed the five detectives and Lieutenant-Colonel Jacobs an hour later, he wagered that all the arrested members of the Committee would break very quickly, "They may be exceptionally ruthless, but they themselves are not the hard men of the security services or the armed forces. While they are probably connected to such people, they are not of this ilk, and they are likely completely demoralized at the rapidity of their arrest and failure of their schemes. A night in the cells contemplating the alternatives placed before them should be enough to produce full cooperation. If it does not, they will be kept until the confinement does soften them up." And with that the Commander asked each of the detectives to describe the arrests that they had made earlier in the afternoon. He stressed that it was important not to ignore or otherwise make light of any deficiencies that came to light in carrying out the plans, "The purpose is not to assign blame for any mistakes; the purpose is to learn from our mistakes so they are unlikely to be made again, and we can be sure that agains will occur in the future."

John Simmons began with the arrest of Sir Lawrence Forrester at the Forrester, Middleton and Grieve bank, "There was nothing unexpected or untoward. The surveillance team had done their job perfectly, and we had an accurate mapping of the bank building and possible exits, as well as the location of the Managing Director's office. As with the other arrests, this came from information collected by the fire services and other public bodies, but they were not informed why we needed the information. My team secured the exits and the front desk of the bank, and I along with other officers proceeded immediately to the office of the managing director, where Forester was behind his desk reading some documents. He was surprised at our entrance without warning and even more so when I cautioned and charged him with murder. However, he put up no opposition and said only, 'I have done my duty as I saw it'. I then led him out of the building quiet as a lamb into a police van that brought him back to the Yard in an escort by the traffic division of the Metropolitan police, who ensured a relatively unimpeded journey for all. It was an ideal arrest, and he behaved in a quiet and dignified way throughout."

Gordon Sinclair followed with an outline of the arrest of Sir Robert Middleton, "In this case the arrest was a bit more complex, given the size of the Home Counties Association building in which Middleton operated. However, as in the previously described case, we had good information as to layout, exits and possible location of the suspect. We secured the reception area and exits of course. However, in proceeding to Middleton's office, he saw us coming along the corridor and, perhaps anticipating danger, quickly disappeared behind one of the doors leading to an exit. But since we had taken the precaution of locating officers throughout the routes of possible escape, he went straight into the strong arms of Constable Smith, and I arrested him forty seconds later. He put up no further opposition, and like Forrester maintained his composure as best he could, but he said nothing. We had prepared the arrest very well, and it was carried out efficiently. He was transported to the Yard in a police van with the route secured by the traffic department of the Metropolitan police, as with Forrester."

Harry Brown then outlined the arrest he and his team had made, "Much the same story is true of the capture of Fraser Elliot, but there was a funny side to the matter in which the dignity and composure of the suspect was seriously compromised, although not deliberately so by me or the other officers. The operation was a large one given the size and complexity of Artful Productions, but everything was well prepared just as with the other cases so far reported. We had excellent information on the layout of the whole complex and the most likely locations of Elliot himself. However, Elliot was not in his office as we expected him to be. His secretary informed us that he had gone to the lavatory and had been there for some time. When we there went and located him in the only cubicle whose door was closed, we found him with his trousers down doing his business. The empirical evidence then released suggested that he had imbibed a large meal of South Asian origin the evening before". At this point, several detectives laughed, but it became clear very quickly that the Commander was not amused, and it ceased immediately. Harry Brown continued, "Nonetheless, my officers maintained their composure, and I cautioned and arrested him there and then. He was, of course, allowed to clean himself and wash his hands, after which he was transported rapidly out of the building to our arresting vehicle. There were plenty of surprised people *en route*, but, other than a lot of gawking, there was nothing out of the ordinary. It was a textbook operation apart from the micro circumstances of the arrest itself, and, twenty minutes later, he was relocated to the cells of Special Branch at the Yard courtesy of an escort provided once again by traffic division of the Met."

Eric Fowler came next and reported on the arrest of Charles Olivier at the City Galleries: "This was a little trickier case. As with the Home Counties Association and

Artful Productions, the Gallery is an exceptionally large building, and we knew that Olivier was not typically in his office as he took a great interest in the details of the presentations of the art. In particular, he had the habit of visiting the various exhibitions and taking a hands-on approach to the placement of the pieces. As a consequence, I had officers on all floors and in all galleries on the lookout for him. Our surveillance team had provided excellent photographs for identification purposes, and all my officers were well prepared to recognize him and communicate with the rest of the team. Sergeant MacPherson did so from Gallery 12, reporting that Olivier was currently engaged there. I and several other officers immediately proceeded to that location. No problems then followed, but when I cautioned and arrested him there, it was not without an element of irony. He was admiring Caravaggio's picture of David with the head of Goliath held in his left hand! The picture had just arrived, on loan from the Galleria Borghese in Rome for several months. However, Olivier proved to be neither a David or a Goliath himself and put up no opposition. He was as quiet as a lamb. As with the other arrests just reported, everything went smoothly and expeditiously. All our planning paid off handsomely, and he has joined his colleagues in the cells below, courtesy once again of an escort from our colleagues in traffic."

Finally, Beth provided her account of the apprehending of James Grieve, "The arrest of Grieve was not quite so straightforward as those of my colleagues. As I made evident earlier, I was worried that we lacked enough information on what would be Grieve's exact location and the opportunities for escape to guarantee success. That is why I requested that we have SAS assistance, and it proved to be most appropriate. Lieutenant-Colonel Jacobs headed the unit and is presently with us now to answer any questions. The house in Hampstead was large, with many exits and the so-called gardens were more like jungles. When we entered the house to make the arrest, we knew he was there, but one of the servants must have sent a warning signal of some kind, and he was able to make an escape from the house into the rear garden. However, our planning was good, and he was apprehended by the SAS. I will ask Colonel Jacobs to explain the details of what happened."

Jacobs rose and spoke to the issue very concisely albeit not without a degree of humour, "As Chief Inspector Hamilton has just explained, Mr. Grieve made an exit into the rear garden where ten of my men had been placed. Sergeant Jenkins saw him first and ordered him to stop, which he did whilst pulling out a pistol and aiming it at the Sergeant. This was a very silly thing to do, especially when Sergeant Jenkins was no more than ten feet away. The Sergeant can move extremely rapidly and is the absolute best I have seen in disarming an opponent. Consequently, I fear that Mr. Grieve has a dislocated right arm and is somewhat shaken up. I do apologize as I had guaranteed that we could apprehend without injury. Nonetheless, the damage was minimal, and the whole experience will likely make the suspect more accommodating. He is actually more shocked than injured, which if you had ever seen the Sergeant in operation would not surprise you." Some of the detectives laughed, and even the Commander had a smile on his face.

Beth then stood up again, thanked the Colonel and requested that he convey the thanks of Special Branch to Sergeant Jenkins himself. She then concluded her presentation, "I made the arrest as soon as I was informed of Grieve's location, and his servants have also been brought in for questioning regarding any warning that they may have sent to James Grieve. I do not know if there will be any charges laid against them, but I suspect not. They are very unlikely to have been privy to the plans and actions of the

Committee and probably saw themselves as doing no more than their duty. Grieve was transported to the Yard in a police helicopter accompanied by Lieutenant-Colonel Jacobs, Constable Wilson and myself. The two servants came by police car and have just arrived."

Beth then sat down, and the Commander began to summarize how things presently stood. As he finished, Andrei walked into the room looking considerably more refreshed than he had earlier that morning. But before he could even acknowledge the greetings of the detectives, Lieutenant-Colonel Jacobs stood up again and exclaimed, "My God, Andrei Chekhov! What on earth are you doing here?". And with that the two men walked toward each other and embraced like long lost brothers. It is difficult to describe the shock on the faces of everyone else in the room, but it subsequently transpired that the two men had been part of an international special forces unit in Mali some years earlier and had worked together for several months fighting ISIS. However, beyond that morsel of information neither of the Colonels would say more.

The Commander's reaction spoke for all concerned when opined, "It really is a small world and also an interconnected one. Hopefully, our success with the assistance of the two colonels will make it even more so. What has been accomplished by those in this room today has been a model of cooperation. Let us all hope it continues and blossoms on all fronts." The Commander then invited one and all to *Holmes and Watson* pub for celebratory drinks and a light supper.

However, in saying all this, Charles Ryder was reminded once again of a concern he had over what appeared to be a developing relationship between Beth and Andrei. He knew that they had spent as much time together as possible since meeting in Moscow, and he had seen how they looked at each other, which suggested that their feelings went beyond those of friendship. Of course, a brief affair would not be a serious problem, but, if they fell in love, this could result in significant changes in the life of both of them, and he certainly did not want to lose Beth from Special Branch. All of the detectives were incredibly good, but she was by far the best. He had worked with her for three years now, and his admiration of her abilities and judgement had risen continually. Obviously, she would not remain under his command for much longer as she was sure to gain promotion very soon. Nevertheless, this did not stop him wanting to keep her as long as possible. His cases were typically difficult and, knowing he always had her on his team, made him less stressed. He also liked her and always found her company interesting and enjoyable, although, unlike many other men, he had no amorous ambitions. That may very well have been different if he were not married to Charlotte, but, as it was so, it was she who was the focus of all his love and devotion.

***

The evening at the pub was full of conviviality as the detectives got on with each other very well and were all incredibly grateful to the two Colonels for their assistance in ensuring a supremely successful operation. Beth was, as usual, popular since she was always good company, as well as easy on the eye for all the other men there. So, she talked to everyone present during the evening including Andrei. However, his company was in even higher demand than her own, so she had to make do without him nearby for most of the evening. On the whole this was not a huge loss to her as she had spent much time with him since his coming to the UK. Just as he had taken care to make her visit to Moscow as pleasant as possible, so she had reciprocated while he had been in London, and the bulk of her free time had been devoted to making his stay as comfortable and enjoyable as could be, aided by an expense account provided by the Commander on which constraints were not specified. She also realized that this was far from being a burden as Andrei was as excellent a company in London as he had been in Moscow and, from her perspective, also extremely easy on the eye. Not surprisingly then, apart from her job, her mind never strayed far from thinking of Andrei, and she was well prepared to appreciate the import of a remark made by Lieutenant-Colonel Jacob's during her conversation with him. Indeed, much later, she realized that it may have been those few words from Jacobs which had set her on a path that had changed her whole life.

The SAS Colonel was still in a state of exhilaration at meeting Andrei again, and, while he would say nothing of their operation in Mali, he was most forthcoming on the character of Andrei himself, and it was this that proved so crucial, "He is a man you can trust. There is no dissembling with him, as one might expect given his present occupation. Those who work for the intelligence services throughout the world are typically people who are the very other of what they seem. But this is not the case with Andrei. He is as straight as a dye and saved my bacon at great danger to himself at least twice when we worked together. There is no one I would trust more once he has made a commitment. I've invited him to visit my home in Hereford and meet the family as he is thinking of continuing his stay in the UK for a couple of weeks in order to take a holiday and my rotation out of London back to our main base will begin tomorrow. My commanding officer would likely not approve of the invite to Andrei for obvious reasons, but some loyalties and obligations take precedence, as they do most definitely in this case."

# VII REMAINS

Charles and Charlotte Ryder were having a leisurely breakfast the following day; it seemed the first for an awfully long time. But the conversation remained centred on the recent events. Charles had just received a telephone call informing him that all the Committee members had signed the confession papers, and he in turn had passed on this information to the Cabinet Secretary's principal assistant who would relay the information to Sir Richard when he came into the office. The protests in the streets were also continuing, albeit with ups and downs, and Charles asked his wife how long she expected them to continue and with what effects. Her response was as succinct and specific as was usual, "The people are the foundation of the nation and the bonds of this nation are strong, yet a set of destabilizing forces have been let loose by successive governments over the years and been framed by the Committee to engender protests. Normally, structural forces are sufficient to ensure appropriate disciplining of the vast majority of people, but when there is such a corrosion of social relations coupled with what might be called surgical-strikes and a brilliant statement of diagnosis, as was done by the Committee, all manner of resentments can translate into oppositional actions." With this, Charlotte paused and asked, "Shall I go on?"

Charles nodded, "Please do. As always, I am interested in what you have to say."

Charlotte continued, "Stated more concretely, neo-liberal economic policies and especially financialization have made many people's lives less secure and contributed massively to the large increase in inequality that is so evident. And there have been multiple accelerants spreading discontents on these bases, including two financial crises and the economic effects of Covid 19. This was given an eloquent expression in the statement of the Committee and coupled to their radical actions has provided the sparks that fired all the combustible material, and which has brought 'the political' into the centre of the frame of reference of the authorities. Now the government has the problem of how they portray the members of the Committee that they have under arrest, but in whatever way they do this I doubt if tranquil conditions will be completely reestablished any time soon. In short, there was much truth in the Committee's statement, and people responded to this. I strongly suspect that the government will initiate a program of reform very soon after they consider order beginning to be restored. This will not be a radical reordering, but it will involve a more regulated capitalism, a more communal liberalism and a party democracy with the fulcrum shifted inward toward the national. Wouldn't you agree?"

To which Charles smiled and responded, "As Sir Ian Richardson so frequently said in his portrayal of the Prime Minister in the television series *House of Cards*, 'You might think that. I could not possibly comment'." His smile broadened as he added, "I am but a functionary attempting to support the reestablishment of order in the moment of 'decision'. And my job is almost done. I have only to tie up some loose ends, ensure the professional interrogators are more fully briefed, and the team and I can relax, or at least take a back seat for some time until a new assignment arrives."

At which point, his phone rang with a call from the Cabinet Secretary. Sir Richard spoke immediately on the

Commander answering, "The Prime Minister has returned and would like you and your team of detectives, as well as your wife and Colonel Chekhov, to come to Number 10 for celebratory drinks at 4.00 p.m. today. Would this be convenient?"

"Most assuredly so sir. That is very good of the Prime Minister. My team and I will appreciate it immensely."

"Excellent Commander. I will see you then," and the Cabinet Secretary rang off.

Turning to Charlotte, Charles smiled again, "I am to inform you that the Prime Minister requires your presence at Number 10 at 4.00 p.m. this afternoon. My team of detectives and Andrei have also been summoned."

"That is exceptionally good news for you my darling!" exclaimed Charlotte, "I shall try to be on my best behaviour and not offend anyone with awkward questions and even more awkward answers. But, while it is just the two of us, I should point out that your investigation has been exceedingly lucky. There was first the photo of Gilchrest's killer, then wholesome cooperation by the FSB, and, if I may say so, my own analysis of the Committee's text that pointed you toward the perpetrators of the killings."

The response from Charles did not propose any serious disagreement but also went beyond what Charlotte had said, "Of course, we were lucky and in the multiple ways you mentioned. But all investigations involving crimes involving intelligence depend on luck of some kind to make the connections that resolve the puzzles presented and end in bringing the villains to justice. Everything you say is true, but, if the luck we actually had never appeared, there may well have been other forms of luck that would have led us to the same end, although most likely it would have been less potent and taken us very much longer to solve the case. Modern policing is incredibly systematic and thorough, and while much of the work subsequently turns out to be a waste of time, sometimes discovering just a sliver of information is the key to the resolution of the mystery and the overall approach pays off. Thus, so it may be in the case of Rory Candiman who was murdered in the morning after his sex party. All present at the party were traced and brought in for questioning, and their fingerprints and DNA samples were taken. This left some prints and samples of DNA found in the apartment unaccounted for. When combined with CCTV footage from the lobby area, this could prove crucial to identifying the killers. Coupled with what Rayevsky told Beth in Moscow as to who the killers might be, we have sent the information to the Spanish and Italian police, as well as several other foreign services, and, hopefully, we will get some useful information from them very soon."

Charlotte's reaction was unusually conciliatory but also shifted the focus to another crucial issue, "Yes, I understand, but ultimate success in this case does depend on speed. After all, as I have just said, there is much truth in the Committee's statement. The truth is put in conservative terms, but much of it could easily be reformulated in social-democratic or socialist form. The effects of neoliberalism and globalization, along with the corrupting effects of modern finance, have been very destructive of the social fabric in Britain. Moreover, the demonstrations and public disorder, which may well be on an upward trajectory, are threatening to the government, and your rapid conclusion of the investigation gives the forces of law and order something to fight back with. It allows them to frame the perpetrators motives and actions in the most disreputable of lights. In other words, the logic of the protests is that a radical political party, or parties, will form and organize the protesters so making them a far more formidable set of forces. After all, remember the remark of the historian Henry Adams that politics is frequently just the 'organization of hatreds', and the Committee's actions have certainly fired up the antagonisms. Being conservatives, I do not think this would have been what the Committee would have had in mind; they probably assumed that popular discontent would have been enough to shift the government onto a fundamentally new Burkean track that was not radical in their view, especially as it is a government of the Conservative Party. However, unintended consequences figure prominently in history. The point remains that a speedy capture of the Committee, and the possibility of thus defaming them provides a chance for the government to survive and reform rather than face radical change."

The Commander smiled, "Again I appeal to the wisdom of Sir Ian Richardson. I am but a functionary administering the Schmittian state of exception my superiors proclaimed." He then blew her a kiss and said he must now go the Yard to begin finishing off the remaining business. But before he got up, he added without a smile, "There is one matter that I most definitely can comment upon; the major piece of luck in this case, as in so much else in my life, is to have met you and for you to have fallen in love with me my darling Charlotte. You are at the centre of my whole being, and I am the most fortunate of men that this is so." With that he got up, kissed her, and said, "Bye for now, see you about 3.30 p.m. at the Yard, just before the reception at Number 10 with the decisionists."

***

The Commander met his detectives and Andrei thirty minutes later, informed them of the confessions of all five members of the Committee and of the invitation to Number 10 Downing Street, both of which was received very favourably by all concerned. He then proposed that they continue with the business of the day, end this at 1.30 p.m., which would allow a couple of hours for everyone to make themselves presentable for their political masters and meet at the Yard again at 3.30 p.m., so they could proceed together to Number 10, courtesy of traffic division once more. There was general nodding of agreement, so he passed on to business. He repeated that all five members of the Committee had confessed to their crimes, and the requisite documents had been signed in front of witnesses. But he now added that no mention was made of the motives or modalities employed in the crimes, and for reasons he had explained yesterday. He also pointed out that, as he had hypothesized yesterday, "They did not have the bottle to resist awfully long."

Charles Ryder then moved to the work that still needed to be done on the investigations, "We must determine if any auxiliary persons were involved in the assassinations, including getting details on all those who actually carried out the killings. Thus, the interrogations of the five members of the Committee is the principal task to be organized. We have access to professional interrogators who already know a great deal about the case but also require further briefings by us. In addition, there is a need to continue organizing the search of the houses and business premises of those we have arrested in order to gather even more information. Anything of relevance we gain can also be put to Rayevsky in Moscow if we need to, as we still have the services of Andrei. There are, of course, also the continuing problems of public order, but we are not responsible for dealing with these. I think another day or two of the same kind of intense activity we have undertaken in the last week should be sufficient to get most matters done for which we are liable. And, just to make things absolutely clear regarding the reception today, all of us can have a couple of hours off beforehand to prepare and will meet again here as a group, together with my wife Charlotte, at 3.30 p.m. We really do deserve a great many thanks from our political masters, and I believe they know this very well."

There were no questions, and all the detectives went about their business once again. Only Andrei was free of responsibilities, so he approached the Commander and said he was off to St. Paul's Cathedral and other notable locales in order to take in some of the sights of London but would be back well before 3.30 p.m.

"Of course," responded the Commander, "I really hope you enjoy the day. You certainly deserve too. I do not know what we would have done without your help. If there are any urgent issues arising, I will call you on your mobile. But I do not expect anything that cannot wait until a more convenient time. So please relax and enjoy yourself. London is a magnificent city in so many ways. And, as a small gesture of my personal thanks to you, here is a new copy of the AA tourist guide to the city that I picked up this morning, and which is excellent. Indeed, it is useful even to people such as me who have lived here most of our lives."

After this the Commander then visited each of the Committee members with the arresting detective and the professional interrogator assigned. All those arrested appeared to remain in a state of shock, which was hardly surprising given the speed with which they had been caught and the huge change in their circumstances over the last twenty-four hours. Lives of privilege and affluence, as well as respect from others, had been replaced by the cells of Special Branch and by the prospect of an unpleasant future for the rest of their lives. The most severely affected was James Grieve, no doubt caused in large part by his encounter with Sergeant Jenkins from which he showed little sign of recovering. However, Forrester did show some spirit by launching into a diatribe against government policies in recent decades, and how the Conservative Party in particular had lost its way and needed, as he put it, a "corrective nudge." The narrative was predominantly Burkean, claiming that the country began its decline under Mrs. Thatcher, continued under her conservative successors and was also extended under Tony Blair and Gordon Brown, the Labour Party prime ministers. And, he added, while the overall plan had failed with their arrests, all the Committee members could take much satisfaction from the public protests against government policies of recent decades. These had been expected to some degree but were far more energetic and widespread than they had imagined possible and were therefore especially heartening.

Charles Ryder did not interrupt him, but when he had finished, Ryder responded by requesting information on the identities of the assassins, as he had with the other four Committee members. Before allowing any reply from Forrester, he also pointed out what he had to the other members of the Committee when he had questioned them, that all their homes and business premises were being subject to thorough searches, along with their computers and phones, and there were also other means by which the validity of any information provided could be checked. He also reminded Forrester, as he had each of the Committee members, of what he had said shortly after all five of the Committee had been arrested regarding their fates if they cooperated and if they did not. In addition, he repeated that it was most unlikely that Forrester or other members of his group would ever see the inside of a court room, or receive any other form of due process, even though both were part of the British system that they sought to rejuvenate. The Commander did not enjoy making these threats, and he knew that several of his team of detectives would likely disapprove somewhat. But he accepted that he had to carry out orders, and that there was a logic to the matter which he understood even if he disliked it.

Forrester, as the chief organizer of the Committee's activities, knew the most with regard to names, payments, contact particulars and likely locations of the assassins. He showed no reticence in providing the information, referring to the assassins as "scum of the earth" at one point, and adding that in this respect they resembled most of their victims. The Commander recorded the information and would contact the police forces in the countries where the killers were thought to be, and with requests that they be arrested immediately on locating them. This would supplement the information already provided on the basis of Rayevsky's interview with Beth, and reinforce the previous requests that arrests be made. But he also knew that it was likely that further information would be provided when the professional interrogators got into their stride very shortly. Nonetheless, it remained true that the bulk of his task and those of his team had been completed, and it was mainly only the paper work that remained to be finished, which would then form the basis of his report to the Commissioner of the Metropolitan Police.

In addition, before leaving those arrested, Charles Ryder also informed all of them that information on links between Committee members and personnel in MI5, MI6 and GCHQ would also be required in short order. This would not be a matter for Special Branch to handle, and other authorities would soon be visiting them to probe into the issues. They, too, would have information to hand that allowed the checking of what was said and not said. Moreover, as at present, the Committee members would remain isolated and would have no way of finding out what the others would say. Thus, it was in the interests of all to tell the truth as they knew it.

There was one final matter that the Commander returned to a couple of hours later and alone. He had had Charlotte's analysis of the Committee's political identity transcribed but with no identification as to who had made it or commented on it. He provided this to Forrester, asked him to read it closely and then convey his views as to its accuracy. He did explain that Forrester was under no obligation to do so, but, if he obliged, Charles promised to mention the cooperation in his report to the Commissioner of the Metropolitan police, and the cooperation would be taken into account in determining his future.

Forrester took the sheets of paper and studied them for several minutes, rereading several passages. Finally, he looked up, smiled and said, "This is amazing. If I had had access to it prior to writing the statement sent to the media last Friday, I would have included parts of it. It is an incredibly accurate description of our political orientation and objectives. Whoever they are, your analysts should be congratulated. I had assumed in writing the statement sent to the media that such political intelligence had become virtually extinct in recent decades and, therefore, saw no danger in writing as I did. Clearly, that was a mistake, and it is part of my undoing. However, there is a bright side, albeit one wholly overshadowed by my present predicament; learning and intelligence regarding politics still prevails in some parts of British institutions".

The Commander then asked Forrester why the particular five bankers that were assassinated were picked rather than others. The reply was straightforward, "Well, the choice was a wide one. All those killed were guilty of multiple malpractices in finance, but, truly, there were many other similar people to pick from. And, if you do not already know let me enlighten you, we had back up assassination plans for other targets if any of our first choices failed or had to be abandoned due to danger to innocents." Charles Ryder nodded, requested, and received the requisite information on the back-up assassins and their targets, and then thanked Forrester for his cooperation. He saw no new problems because what Forrester had said was consistent with the information provided by Rayevsky, or otherwise deduced, and no members of The Committee now had any incentive to lie.

On his way back to E wing, where the offices of the investigation were located, he met with Andrei, who he had not expected to see for a considerable time. He expressed surprise, "Was St. Paul's and the rest of London not to your taste?"

"No, no", responded Andrei, "St, Paul's was magnificent. It was the demonstrations in central London that were the problem. They are continuing as vibrant as ever, and it was exceedingly difficult to walk anywhere else, so I decided to come back and relax. The Committee may well be neutralized, but the effect of their actions has not."

Charles nodded, "It would seem so. We may well be living in a changing age. Ultimately, the Committee could turn out to have been a catalyst for such, but as yet we do not have much idea of exactly how and to what extent the age will change. Doubtless, there will be many speculating on this, and it will be interesting to observe actual results, but, for my part, at this stage, I do not expect anything really radical will prevail."

When he returned to his office, he communicated the new information he had from Forrester to the office of the Cabinet Secretary and then received four new messages all containing more good news for the investigation. The French police in Lyon had arrested Bin Binot, thought to be the assassin of James Stewart. As long as the evidence presented was sufficiently convincing for a French court, there would be no problem with extradition to Britain because he faced no charges in France. Charles knew that providing such would not be a problem as there was evidence from the shoeprints in the woods and from the Ford Focus pickup vehicle, which had been found the day before, that was sufficient for the purpose of convincing a French court that he was a valid suspect. Vladimir Romanovitch and Ernst Schneideral, who had killed Billy Jones, were also under arrest in St. Petersburg and were available for interview by the British police, either in person or via Skype. The Russian police added that, although there was no extradition treaty with the UK, they would not oppose his relocation to the country if there was a request made. There was, thirdly, a communication from the Spanish police in Madrid that they had recently detained two women, Maria Sanchez and Violeta Piera, whose names were on the list provided by Rayevsky and confirmed by Forrester to be the assassins of Rory Candiman. The Spanish police also reported that their DNA matched the samples provided by Special Branch from those in the apartment in which Rory was murdered, and they also appeared on the CCTV footage sent which attested to their presence at the building at the requisite time. Finally, Rayevsky's two assistants in the assassination of Sir Roger Gilchrest, Ivan Morozovic and Oxana Solomatic, had been located in South Africa and were now in the custody of the Johannesburg police. They faced charges there connected to the illegal possession of weapons, but the South African police added that there should be no major difficulties of extradition if British evidence were compelling, as it would be given the testament of Rayevsky. On reading all four messages, Charles thought to himself, "Very good, indeed, seven out of the eight assassins had been apprehended, along with all the organizers of the assassinations. Not bad for a week's work." He would convey the good news personally to the Prime Minister and Sir Richard at the reception in Downing Street.

Nonetheless, Charles Ryder recognized that the

problems surrounding The Committee's project was far from resolved, even though he also knew there was little more for he and his team to do. True, the assassin of Stephanie Armstrong still had not been located, but the matter had been taken out of his hands. The identity was revealed by Forrester, but Charles had been ordered by Sir Richard not to follow up on this unless the killer could be located in Britain itself. Since it had emerged that the suspect had long departed British shores, nothing further remained for Special Branch to do on the matter. Unlike the other four assassinations, the only evidence available on Stephanie's killer came from The Committee and Ryder surmised that since the government had not yet finalized how it would portray the assassinations and arrests of The Committee, they did not want any reference whatsoever to the latter in any extradition request.

The Commander believed that much the same would prove to be the case with the back-up assassins as the only information and evidence here came from Forrester, so the government would not proceed until they had settled on a narrative covering all events that suited their purposes. And whatever was decided, he did not expect that the consequences would involve more work for Special Branch and himself. Other organs of the state would most likely take over when anything further needed doing. As a policeman, Ryder was uneasy about all this because it did not square with the law he had sworn to uphold, or with the proclaimed nature of democratic government. However, he recollected the analysis he, himself, had provided his own detectives when they had expressed similar reservations. The current situation was not one where legality prevailed; it was a state of exception in which decisionism reigned, so the circumstances were far from normal, and the established rules and procedures did not apply. His flippant remark that morning in talking to Charlotte portraying himself as "but a functionary administering the Schmittian state of exception" was also a true description. This induced a serious degree of discomfort for him, even though he knew he could legitimate his actions in these terms, just as he had done with his detectives the day before. Perhaps if there had not been such widespread protests in support of the Committee's actions, he would have been less bothered, but as it was he now recognized that the legitimacy he claimed in explaining matters to his detectives was insufficient to fully persuade himself. And he strongly suspected that Charlotte would think along similar lines, which bothered him even more. He resolved to speak to her on the matter at a later time.

***

The reception at Number 10, Downing Street began with a short address by the Prime Minister, who was very gracious in his thanks to one and all, and he had the courtesy to mention all of the names of those invited. Beyond this though, he said nothing of substance and looked very tired and 'worn', and he apologized for having to leave shortly as there was business to attend too which he could not postpone. But he also made the point of saying he would talk to each individually during the next hour and express his thanks personally again. He knew everyone had worked so incredibly hard, and he wanted above all to ensure that one and all knew they had the gratitude of Her Majesty's Government and the British people. And with that, he ended his address and urged everyone to begin enjoying the many refreshments available. He added that there was no time limit in doing so, and his own departure very soon should not be regarded as a signal to end the reception. Sir Richard would remain as host.

As it turned out the event was better than everyone's expectations. Conversations with the detectives, Charlotte and Andrei seemed even to energize the Prime

Minister, and he stayed longer than he had planned as a result. Sir Richard could also be excellent company, and he, too, was genuinely grateful for the speedy completion of the investigation and the apprehension of the principals involved. He thanked one and all individually but was, not unnaturally, most pleased in talking to Charlotte, not only because she was such a beautiful woman, but also because he was so admiring of her intellect and, unlike most others, not frightened by it. He was also quickly taken with Beth, as, indeed, was the Prime Minister himself.

The Commander concentrated his attention on his male detectives and found no burden in doing so. All were intelligent and thorough police officers with excellent records, which is why he had picked them for the investigation. They were also pleasant to talk to informally, being good story tellers and humourous to boot. In particular, they took pride in being police officers, as did he, and there was mutual respect and genuine friendship between them all irrespective of rank. This included Beth as well, but the Prime Minister as well as Sir Richard were spending rather longer in her company, so the men of Special Branch were left to themselves for a more extended time than either Charlotte or Beth..

Nonetheless, each of the principal detectives also made a point of talking to Charlotte to congratulate her on the accuracy of the analysis she had provided to the investigation and to thank her once again. She appreciated this and was very friendly, even extending a favour of her time to the needs of Harry Brown. He had approached her last and begun, "I want to apologize to you Professor."

"What an earth for Chief Inspector?" interjected Charlotte before he could continue.

"Well, I was a bit rude, or at least somewhat dismissive, at the end of your presentation to us at the Yard. You were completely accurate, and I feel such a fool, as well as an oaf."

"Please think nothing of it. I did not take offence, and I believe you articulated a common view of conservatives which I was expecting someone to say. This allowed me to justify my position very clearly, so I am actually grateful to you." Then, she immediately added, "Sorry, that sounds condescending. I did not mean it that way. And all I have heard of you from Charles is positive. He has an extremely high opinion of your abilities, which is why he selected you to be part of the investigation."

"You are actually being very gracious Professor," Harry responded, "so perhaps you will not mind if I raise another subject completely outside the investigation."

"Please feel free."

Harry continued, "My problem in my response to your analysis of the political identity of the assassins is that I never realized how rigorous, how insightful, and how true political theorists could be. And your capabilities here were reinforced later by that of your husband in explaining the political nature of the situation we faced. All this has fundamentally changed my perspective. Until now, I had thought political analysis was just hot air and without substance."

Charlotte interjected, "Much of it is. Indeed, these days the bulk of it seems to be just that."

"Yes, that may be so," Harry continued, "but your analysis was in a different league altogether and has wholly changed my view on the potentialities of informed political analysis, and I am hugely grateful to you for this. And, hopefully, the experience will not just aid me in the future. My daughter, Bronwyn, will be applying for university entrance very soon and intends to study politics as her main subject. She is genuinely clever as all her teachers attest, and she does go to an excellent school. Everyone is sure that she will get acceptance at one of the finest universities and do very well. However, I want her to *understand* political theory as you so clearly do, and, more generally, I want her to be like you and also like Beth, and become an independent, intellectual woman beholding to no opinions contrary to what they believe to be the truth. So, I wonder if you could give her some advice. No one she knows at present, certainly not me, can provide what is needed, and she would be thrilled if you would meet her."

"Of course, I would be glad too," replied Charlotte and then reached into her bag and gave Harry a card, adding, "Here is the telephone number and email addresses of the secretaries to the department of politics at University College. I will mention to them to expect a contact from Bronwyn, and they will arrange a time when she can come and see me in my office or, if she prefers, over coffee. And when we meet, she should not feel rushed. I will make sure that I do not have to be in a hurry. You might mention that to her."

"That is very kind of you Professor."

"Not at all Harry, I remain a traditional academic, quite different from the managerialist and careerist neoliberal varieties that now populate the universities, and, therefore, I am interested in fostering intelligence and learning in students who will later maybe become professors themselves and take over from my generation. In other words, there is a little bit of Burkeanism in me, although I stress it is only a little bit." And smiling she added, "But there is a request I have of you too – please call me Charlotte."

Harry and Charlotte then began to circulate in separate ways, and eventually Charlotte and Andrei began to talk, with Beth and Sir Richard joining them shortly thereafter. And it was not long before Charlotte asked Andrei what he thought it was that had made the Russian government agencies so cooperative and helpful with the British investigation. In particular, she inquired, "Did he believe it was all down to the change in administration under President Kovalny?"

Andrei smiled and replied, "I am incredibly pleased that Kovalny has come to the Presidency, but this is because he has been cleaning up all the corruption that grew in the previous regimes, as well as easing up on the domestic repression that also increased along with the corruption. However, international politics is another issue altogether and more complex because it is not just a matter affecting the Russian government, as you yourself and, doubtless, Sir Richard and Beth know very well. However, it may be useful if I spell out how the matter is understood by the government in Russia."

"Please do," said Sir Richard, "I would be most interested in what you have to say."

Charles, who had just joined them, also interjected, "That would be of great interest to me as well. So many things, large and small, depend on this". Several of the other detectives who were on the edges of the grouping also nodded.

Andrei took this as his cue, "I will answer in terms of the standard theory of international relations and especially of geopolitics. The theory may not be universally valid, but many believe it is, and even more believe it applicable to current circumstances. This includes the Russian government. So, let us first begin with two basics of the theory. First, interstate relations do not take place in a realm of effective law as relations between people do in most modern states, and the international situation is, therefore, often described as 'anarchic'. Second, the prime concern of any state is maintaining itself as independent, so security trumps everything else, including economic growth and prosperity. Now consider the situation of Britain. In the 1990s, the Soviet Union collapsed along with the ideological and military threats posed by the 'East' to the 'West', and American hegemony began to fade a couple of decades thereafter. The continent of Europe was thus returned to more traditional geopolitics by these two developments. Moreover, in this context one important change has happened, and another widely expected change did not happen. The change that occurred was Brexit. The UK left the European Union, and now the relations it has with the bloc are pretty much like that of any other nation outside the EU. The change that was expected to happen but did not happen was that the EU did not collapse or even show serious signs of collapse. Quite the contrary in fact, the union appears to be deepening even more, and it is not unreasonable to expect that ultimately a super-state will form in Europe. That is a problem for any, and I do stress *any*, British government."

Andrei paused and took a sip of his wine. He then continued, "Historically, the UK's foreign policy has been geared to stopping a single power dominating the continent of Europe, and the major wars that Britain has been involved in for over two hundred years have always been the result of precluding attempts to unify Europe, most particularly those of Napoléon, Kaiser Wilhelm, and Hitler. In all cases, Russia was an important ally. That is not surprising because Britain's security problem with a unified Europe is exactly the same as Russia's problem with a unified Europe. It too fears for its security in the face of a European hegemonic power and has much historical evidence to make the fear rational, just as Britain has. There is, therefore, a developing concordance of interest between the two countries, and any strengthening of Britain is now welcomed by Russia, just as I suspect is the case with Britain welcoming a better functioning and stronger Russia. There are still one or two points of friction, but I would expect these to be successfully addressed in the near future. Consequently, cooperation is the order of the day, and the day will, I believe, be enduring. What do you think Professor; have I missed something important?"

Charlotte responded instantly, "I could not have put it better myself. The structures of alliances are reforming, and for the very sound reasons you outlined."

Before she could continue, however, Sir Richard intervened and remarked, "That is most interesting Colonel, but let me ask you another question. Assuming you are right about a concordance of interests between Russia and Britain regarding Europe, how do nuclear weapons change matters compared with the past? Both Russia and Britain are nuclear powers, and one might expect in the coming decades that the EU will become so. It does not have to start from square one here as the French of course are nuclear armed and an important member of the European Union, while Germany is a threshold power regarding nuclear weapons. Is not the balance of terror sufficient to keep the peace, thereby making the balance of power theory you work with and alliances based upon it irrelevant? I ask this because I am genuinely interested in your answer and it is a crucially important issue."

"That is an excellent question Sir Richard," responded Andrei, "and as you are no doubt aware, there is no settled answer. Moreover, and, rather fortunately, we lack direct empirical evidence on the matter. But I would make the following observations. Not every war is destined to go nuclear because of the devastating effects that will be inflicted upon the initiator of such a war. Furthermore, power is a variable and other things being equal it is better to have more of it rather than less. There is probably no minimal amount of power that will ensure the security of any country in all circumstances, even if they are nuclear armed. Hence, it is also better to have allies than not have them. Furthermore, if conflict, even war, does occur, what does victory mean? I suggest it means exactly what it has always meant, the capacity to impose a *political* settlement on the defeated. Again, then, more power is better than less power, and having dependable and powerful allies is better than being alone or relying on undependable allies. Thus, I think Britain and Russia will draw closer together in the coming years and that it will be an enduring alliance and friendship because the structural conditions that underpin it will persist."

Sir Richard continued immediately on Andrei finishing, "That is exceedingly interesting indeed. I would only respond by saying that you are not alone in thinking along such lines, and I believe it would be highly beneficial if you conveyed this to members of the Russian government. I doubt if they would be surprised, but it may reassure them that British opinion tends to be analogous to their own." He then turned to Charlotte and said, "I do sincerely apologize my dear for interjecting into your conversation with Colonel Chekhov, but it was an opportunity for clarification and bettering even further our relations with Russia that I did not want to miss."

"Not at all Sir Richard. I was about to ask much the same question as yourself and appreciate that you asked it because, while it does not change its intellectual import, you asking it and your response to the answer are much more likely to have real and beneficial effects. But let us also ask Beth what she thinks of all these matters. She has been silent so far, but she has a keen intellect, and I know she keeps up with the current events and knows political theory and history extremely well."

Charlotte was not disappointed by Beth's reaction and nor were the others, although she did begin cautiously,

"I do not think I can add anything of substance, but from all the politics and history classes I took at Kings College, along with what I have learned subsequently, what has been said makes a great deal of sense, and some of it is of long standing. Remember, for example, Palmerston in 1848 in the House of Commons remarked, 'We have no eternal allies, and we have no perpetual enemies. Our interests are eternal and perpetual, and those interests it is our duty to follow.' So, I too concur with what Andrei has said about a geopolitical concordance of interests between Britain and Russia in the present circumstances, and its likely continuance. Furthermore, I believe that what he has said about what victory means in the context of state conflict is but an application of Clausewitz's now classic work *On War*. However, this said, there is also one important matter that has so failed to receive due consideration, namely the orientation of the United States."

She paused for a moment to collect her thoughts, and then continued, "The country still has a potential to be enormously powerful, but it is well into the process of losing global hegemonic status, and the exact foreign policy positions have not been clear for some years apart from attempts to contain China. This relative decline of the United States arose principally because the American business class favoured integrating China into the world economy, so facilitating its rapid development, while the Pentagon's concern with the geopolitical implications were devalued until the last few years or so. And this focus of American business on outsourcing much production to China did huge economic damage to a significant portion of the American working class in so-called heartland states, making them susceptible to populisms of the radical right. This has also been joined by them embracing conspiracy theories that claim the country is being undermined by an array of progressives, or what many Americans seem to think are really communists. No doubt these developments have been fanned by demagogues using social media, but there are also much deeper roots at work too."

Beth paused again, and Sir Richard responded to what she had said by asking, "What exactly are these deeper roots?"

"I think they partly hinge on the fact that the civil war of the late nineteenth century was never properly settled, again in terms of understanding victory in Clausewitz terms," answered Beth. "In other words, the North did not succeed in imposing a *political* settlement on the South that would integrate it *fully* with the North and West of the country. This would have required redistributing the land of former slaveowners to blacks and poor whites so creating a large middle class similar to those in the rest of the country, and, moreover, one that was multi ethnic so that the interests of blacks and whites would converge, but this was not done. And neither was there a serious enduring attempt to include blacks into the electorate, so much voter suppression remains to this day. As a consequence, the civil war never really ended, and the conditions underlying it have only been modified not eliminated. Thus, conflict flares up repeatedly every now and then, and presently the flare ups appear to be on a rising curve due to the factors I have already mentioned. And I suspect that they could become even more serious, especially as the bulk of Latinos are recent immigrants to the United States and have not forgotten that much of the south and west of the country was stolen from their forefathers.'

Beth paused again to catch her breath, and then continued, "On top of all this there are the effects of climate change, which appear to be particularly severe for many parts of the United States that presently have large populations and require new government programs that are opposed in other parts of the United States. Furthermore, in recent decades a new high-tech economy has emerged in some coastal states, so the differences from so-called 'fly-over' states become even larger, and underpin divergences of progressives and conservatives, so further intensifying internal conflicts. Indeed, when all the dots are joined, one might hypothesize that there could be a process underway of systemic fragmentation and division, and perhaps portending collapse in the United States analogous to Hemingway's characterization of bankruptcy, 'it takes place gradually, then suddenly.' This is made more likely by the fact that the US also appears to have more than its fair share of air heads, and the popular cultures everywhere, North and South, West and East, are particularly dire and include a propensity to accumulate weaponry and form militias that is further destabilizing."

Again, Beth stopped, this time to sip more wine, then went on, "Nonetheless, whatever happens, it is possible that America will also see the EU as a strategic threat, especially if it cozies up to China. Such dominance of Eurasia, or the 'world island' as Halford Mackinder described it, would not be acceptable to America under any circumstances. However, I would like to conclude on another dimension of international relations. It would be far better for the vast bulk of people if states learned from history and engineered effective collective security institutions. These could overcome the competition and conflict generated under conditions of 'anarchy' which Andrei described. However, and much to my disappointment, the lessons of history do not appear to have much impact generally, including on this matter."

Andrei reacted immediately, "That was really insightful and in all respects".

For his part, Sir Richard responded, "I see that the talents of Special Branch detectives extend well beyond their legislated duties, and that is heartening to know. If you ever think of a new career, I believe the British Foreign Office would be extremely interested, and I would be more than willing to support you on a relocation."

The Commander looked horrified at this prospect but said nothing. For her part, Charlotte simply offered an invitation, "Yes, indeed, I would like all three of you to come to my 3 o'clock graduate seminar tomorrow afternoon. The topic is international politics; the students are exceptionally good, and all of you are even better."

Sir Richard was the first to respond, "I would really love too, but my position as Cabinet Secretary would not allow it. I have probably been far too free with my views already, but the company was so stimulating I could not help myself and lost the reserve that is expected of me. However, I will be retiring very soon, and if your invitation is extended then, I will be an enthusiastic respondent."

Beth followed, "I, too, am sorry and have to decline Charlotte." And smiling at Charles continued, "My boss is exceptionally good and understanding as you know, but he has already assigned me some tasks that must be completed by the end of the day after tomorrow."

Charlotte looked a little down and just said, "But we really must have lunch together again very soon".

Beth smiled, "Of course, we must. I look forward immensely to our chats, and I really need your advice on a couple of matters."

Charlotte's spirits were raised again, however, when Andrei said in response to the invitation, "I would enjoy that very much indeed."

# VIII RENEWALS

After the reception ended, Charles and Charlotte decided to walk at least part of the way home to Gower Street. Protests appeared to have subsided somewhat this Friday evening, so while the streets were sometimes busy, they were not impossibly so. Charles took the opportunity to ask Charlotte for clarification of her views on the matter of closeness in relationships of all kinds, including friendships of people as well as alliances between states. He was still thinking of his remark regarding cooperation between the quite different people involved in the investigation and in particular of Beth and Andrei.

Charlotte's response was both reassuring and unnerving, "Of course, friendship between individuals can be based on multiple factors ranging from a shared sense of humour to romantic love. But, typically, structural factors, or if you prefer other words, social relationships, will be involved too. Being part of the same network of connections among a wider set of people where hostilities are scarce or mild would be a highly supportive factor. And in its absence, there would doubtless be more stresses and strains that acted corrosively on those involved or brought major changes in their lives. Moreover, and unfortunately, it is most unlikely that such a network of solidarities can encompass all people or, in the case of international relations, all countries. There are too many bases of division to form, including the fact – and it does appear to be a fact – that closer relations between A, B, and C tend to mean fewer close relations with, say, D, E and F. In other words, closer relations between some can generate fewer close relations with others. The factors involved in personal relationships are different from those between political entities, but analogous processes are at work."

After a slight pause, Charlotte continued, "I suppose that your question involves a matter close to home. In particular, I think you are wondering about Beth and Andrei. You have mentioned to me several times over the last few days about how attached they appear to have become, and you worry that this might mean losing Beth from Special Branch or even the police service generally. After all, Andrei is an officer of the Russian secret service, and, even if he resigned the post, this would not allay all the fears of the authorities that his having a relationship with a senior Special Branch detective would be dangerous for security. This would likely be the case even if the UK and Russia become close allies. And, of course, you do not want to lose her, not only because you like her, but because she is your best officer and a friend of mine. Am I not right?"

"Of course, you are right. You invariably are," responded Charles. "I am genuinely concerned about the matter, even though I admire both Beth and Andrei and really do wish all the best for them both. And it is not just that Beth would have to leave Special Branch and probably the police altogether; Andrei would have to undergo similar changes because the security concerns of the Russian government would be analogous to those of the British. This would be true even if Britain and Russia do become close allies as they would remain separate states, and trust in other states, no matter how friendly, is limited. Thus, if they are falling in love, it does not bode well for either of them as it will prove so fundamentally disruptive of the lives they have now."

"Yes, that could be true", replied Charlotte, "but there is a silver lining in the cloud. The macro situation typically impacts on the micro, so changes in geopolitical and societal relations impact and mold the opportunities available in individual lives. While those of Andrei and Beth will alter as you say, if Britain and Russia do actually continue to become closer this will make adjustment for both of them very much easier than it would be if the two countries were hostile to each other. Thus, it is much more likely that other good ways of living will open up for them. Doubtless, both Beth and Andrei recognize this. So, it should also comfort you to some extent if you really do wish them all the best, and at least there is no chance that an intervention by Sir Richard will lead to you losing Beth to the Foreign Office!"

Charlotte paused momentarily before adding, "And mentioning Sir Richard also should remind us that Beth now has a powerful friend, or at least an influential contact, which would likely allow smoothing out any difficulties that arise in a deeper relationship with Andrei. Sir Richard also has a debt to Andrei himself which reinforces the point. So, all in all, I do not think it will be catastrophic for them if Beth and Andrei become a couple."

"Well, if Beth and Andrei do decide to have a permanent relationship, I hope you are right," acknowledged Charles, "but there is also a much larger topic on which I need your advice. I have misgivings about my role in the investigation that is now nearly complete. It has involved actions that will likely facilitate political misrepresentations on a major scale by the government and are not, therefore, wholly legitimate. I can go into details when we get home, but I, suspect, you know the kind of issues that are causing me some angst."

"Yes, I think, I might," answered Charlotte. "But I also suspect that you know that I cannot be much help. Both the domain of action, or the exercise of power, and that of values are complex and typically involve contradictions. There are no actions whose intended outcomes can be assured, and actual outcomes will likely include negative as well as positive effects when assessed by any set of values, and, of course, there are many different sets of values. Thus, there is always a multiplicity of contrary effects in the exercise of power, and in their normative assessment. Moreover, even when a particular set of values is chosen to assess alternative actions, there are no obvious rules allowing the determination of what is the best choice overall by reducing the multitude of effects of each to a common quantitative measure that can be added and then compared. Sorry to be so negative, but that is the way realities are. We can certainly discuss matters in a more concrete way when we have privacy at home, and I would be interested in doing so as I have been involved in the investigation too. However, given what I have just said, I am not optimistic that we will resolve much. The only basis for reassurance is that this is the situation generally; it is not just a problem for us in the here and now."

"Yes, I understand what you say," answered Charles, "but it is small comfort to me, and I, suspect, for you too."

"True," continued Charlotte, "I know, as you know, that this is not sufficiently reassuring. Like Beth, we want more and entertain the notion that if people had greater rationality, or better knowledge, or more control of their lives, this could result in a significantly improved world. Such hopes appear to be part of the human condition, my love, but so also is critical thought and the destruction of illusions."

"That is really not a satisfactory conclusion at all," answered Charles.

"I agree, but satisfaction is one thing and logic another. And the only way to be sure to attain a harmony between the two in the matter to hand is for people to become wholly routinized. In other words, for each and all persons to occupy a role in a particular structure of relationships that require specific actions determined by an unambiguous rule book or culture. In short, problems disappear if people become robots."

Charles laughed, adding, "That is very clever my darling, but I think there are exceptions to your logic, and we should explore them over dinner when we get home. It is already prepared and just needs heating. Or, perhaps, you think there could be complexities that make such an expectation questionable!"

"No, I think dinner is highly likely exempt from any indeterminacy. And I apologize for being so negative and will behave better over dinner."

Charles responded, "Ah, a chink in the armour. I shall take advantage of this and explain why I believe the government may act illegitimately; a matter my detectives are genuinely concerned about. I managed to calm them down partially, courtesy of Carl Schmitt and some very sensible remarks by Harry Brown, but I also now share some of the reservations they expressed and will relay them to you for your assessment. We have all done our duty so far, but full compliance with the future actions of the present government is another matter entirely, or so I now believe."

At that very moment, a large group of demonstrators appeared at the north end of Trafalgar Square near the National Gallery, most likely on their way to the Parliament buildings. Charles immediately responded by saying, "This looks to be an exceptionally large and determined as well as a boisterous group. We do not want to get caught up in it even though we both may be sympathetic to the cause. Let us take the tube; Charing Cross station is just behind us." Charlotte nodded and replied, "Yes, that is a good idea, but the day may soon come when we have to decide what side we are on and what we are going to do about it, as will your detectives."

***

For their part, after the reception at Number 10 had ended, Andrei and Beth walked together to a French restaurant, *Le Bordeaux*, near the Yard, which they had chosen for dinner that evening.

"How did you find things?" asked Beth.

"Much better than expected actually. I particularly liked the discussion with you, Charlotte and Sir Richard. And I believe Sir Richard really would like it reported to my bosses at the FSB and beyond. I do not believe he said more than he later suggested was appropriate. He wants me to convey his views as those of the British government in order to help reassure the new Russian government that Britain is on the same page as itself. If I thought he genuinely did not want his views known, I would be silent, but Cabinet secretaries do not make such mistakes of misspeaking. They are the consummate professionals, and it will aid Anglo-Russian rapprochement if the relevant people in the Russian government know his views."

"Would you really not report what he said if you believed he had revealed more than he intended?" responded Beth. "When all is said and done, you are an officer of Russian intelligence and, I believe, also a Russian patriot".

"Yes, you describe me accurately. But I also have a personal honour, or, perhaps I  should say, I believe I have a personal honour and try to maintain it, and since I was not tasked with doing anything more than facilitate the investigation of the assassinations, I would have remained silent as to the specific views of Sir Richard. However, as I said, I believe Sir Richard really does want the views he concurred with passed on to the Russian government, and he is right in believing it will facilitate cooperation to the mutual benefit of both countries."

Beth responded, "Well, if we are in the domain of personal honour, I must confess to feeling a bit shabby. I have done my job as best I could in this investigation, but as a 'political being', I recognize much in the critique launched by the Committee that is legitimate, although not the violent actions aimed at promoting it. As I now appreciate much more than hitherto, the main thrust of the country's economic policy for the last several decades has been orientated to the benefit of the what we might reasonably call the 'extractive class', particularly those engaged in finance. This has corroded the quality of social relationships and culture generally, as well as individual beliefs and behaviours. Moreover, as I understand matters, trends in the development of artificial intelligence and robotics will make matters very much worse economically for the bulk of people unless policies are substantially changed, and this will devalue their lives even more. I would hate to think that as a police officer I had acted to sustain the current trajectory. One does not have to accept the conservative analysis of the Committee's statement to recognize all this or identify the protests with their Burkean agenda. And even if it is accepted that the analysis of the Committee is substantially correct in the concepts employed, everything could be expressed in terms of an alternative partisanship."

She paused for a moment to step aside in the face of a large group of people walking in the other direction and seemingly unaware of anyone else's existence. After they had passed, she continued, "I know at least some of my colleagues probably experience the same uneasiness and, like me, have not been especially vocal about it. Both Charles and Charlotte Ryder are far too intelligent and worldly wise not to be in at least two minds about what has happened and their roles in supporting the authorities. But I suppose they, again like me, have felt dominated by the logic of the positions they hold or in the case of Charlotte by that of her husband's position. In any event, they go with the flow, while I am beginning to think that on this matter, I would prefer to be something of a counter-current or at least a blockage or at a minimum not to be involved, which of course is impossible given my present position.  Thus, I am now more than a little divided as to my role in the investigation, and the police more generally, and wonder whether I should seriously consider getting a new career. There is no doubt that my orientation has been changed somewhat by the investigation. As Nietzsche would put it, a 'revaluation of values' may be called for.

"What do you mean exactly? I appreciate what Nietzsche meant in the context of his time, but what do you mean?" asked Andrei.

"Well, in a nutshell, I had assumed that there were two basic conditions for people to attain genuine agency and fashion themselves as they would wish to be: democracy and an established legal order. Of course, for the two conditions to be effective requires the absence of major external threats to the country, such as Russia experienced in its 'concentrated history' for much of the twentieth century, and a living standard well above the bare minimum. In these circumstances, democracy allows collective choice of the social conditions of life, and maintaining legal order facilitates a genuine choice of individual life projects, or lifestyles, incorporating real value within the state of affairs determined by democracy. However, the actions of the Committee and the reactions of the people in support of their program have revealed serious limitations of British democracy. It appears to have been captured, or subverted, by special interests, and, rather than the police maintaining a legal order that allows people genuine choice over their own lives, the police are required to support an order constructed by these special interests which the protests are showing lack widespread popular support. And this is blatantly clear in the suspension of legality in the state of emergency, or what Schmitt would call the state of exception."

"Yes, I do understand," responded Andrei.

"However, matters may be worse than this," Beth continued, "my confidence in people's capacity to actually choose and construct a worthwhile life-project for themselves has waned. Thus, even if democracy were purified and the dominance of special interests eliminated, I am now less sure that people's agency would be enhanced much. A large section of the populace appears to be committed to air-head activities irrespective of the condition of democracy and the legal order. So, I face something of an existential choice for myself as there are definitely opportunities for a new path with lowered ambitions but likely more achievements. My uncle would be thrilled if I were to come and work in his company, and what he has on offer is extremely attractive in multiple dimensions."

"What does your uncle's company focus on?" asked Andrei.

"My uncle is an engineer and designer and concentrates on making the everyday world of people both more functional and more beautiful simultaneously. He does so by crafting aesthetically pleasing products that are also more efficient, and which everyone uses continually. In short, he attempts to take some of the ugliness and toil out of existence and, thereby, improve the quality of people's lives."

"For what it is worth, my advice is not to make any hasty decisions," answered Andrei, "but, that said, your position is very understandable for me as well. I, too, sometimes think my own occupation often inhibits me from doing what I think should ideally be done. Like you, I entertain the idea of a new activity that would make me more comfortable with life. But uncertainty and inertia are immensely powerful forces, and we really need something new to enter our lives that encourages us to more seriously consider the options we actually face."

"Yes, indeed, but let us really hope for a breaking of the molds," replied Beth, "now how about talking of the really important matters soon to be before us; what do you fancy eating tonight?"

***

After they had sat down in the restaurant and made their orders of food and wine, Beth came to the topic that had been preying on her mind since the previous evening. "I hear you are intending to take a holiday in England. Where do you think you will go?"

Andrei responded, "I am really glad you asked as I didn't know how to broach the subject with you. I have been wondering if it were at all possible for you to join me and show me more of your beautiful country, as well as allowing me the pleasure of even more of your beautiful company."

Beth smiled, paused for a few moments and then said, "Well, as it so happens, you are in luck Colonel. I can and would be happy to do so. I was due to go on holiday the day after the assassinations occurred but was requested by the Commander to postpone it until the investigation of Special Branch was finished. Since this is pretty much the case now, he has just approved my new request for vacation leave. If you can wait a couple of days while I take care of loose ends, we can begin a holiday together on Sunday morning."

"Of course, I can wait two days," said Andrei, with a broad smile on his face.

"Good. I propose we begin at the cottage of my uncle in Stow on the Wold, which is a village in the Cotswolds' area about one hundred miles to the west of London, and it is an extremely attractive place to visit. There is also most unlikely to be any protest activity in the neighbourhood to disrupt us. We can drive there in my car and stay for a few days before travelling elsewhere if you wish. My uncle is currently away on a business trip to Russia of all places, where he is establishing a new division of his company, and he will not be back for several weeks, so it will just be the two of us. I hope that suits."

Andrei reached for her left hand, gently brought it toward himself and kissed it, "Of course, nothing could be better. There is no one I would sooner be with in the whole world."